A STUDY IN PASSION

THE MARRIAGE MAKER

DAUGHERS OF SCANDAL

LOUISA CORNELL

DAUGHTERS OF SCANDAL

The sins of the father are visited upon the children...

One cannot help their circumstances of birth, but even the Most High understands how cruel people can be. As the former ward of a baron and the new Duke of Roxburgh, Sir Stirling James has seen this principal in action within the elite ranks of the *ton*.

Sir Stirling James, Duke of Rothburgh, has one particular weakness—he delights in seeing *Society* in scandal. Nae, he delights in *creating* scandal. And what greater scandal than for The Marriage Maker to introduce into the *ton* four genteel ladies whose fathers' crimes have ostracized them?

CHAPTER 1

OCTOBER *1817*
Edinburgh

SIR THEO GRINDON SORELY NEEDED NEW DRAWERS.

Having one's entire wardrobe shied out the second-floor window of one of the more fashionable addresses in Edinburgh certainly did not constitute a scientific method of study.

Yet, the light of the risen sun did illuminate the flaws in one's drawers to great advantage. The fact these items, along with various other articles of Theo's clothing, now draped the doorstep, shrubbery, pavement, and spiked garden gate before Number 14 Charlotte Square illuminated another set of flaws.

His own.

Two threadbare portmanteaus landed on the pavement with a resounding *thump*.

"Isn't it customary to pack one's clothing *into* one's luggage before leaving a lady's residence?"

Theo suppressed a groan. Of all the people to witness his latest precipitous eviction, Sir Stirling James was the *last* person he expected or wanted to be about this early in the morning. The man was a duke, for God's sake. Weren't there rules against dukes, even Scottish ones, leaving their beds before noon? With a half-hearted attempt at a smile, Theo turned to greet his old friend.

"I was not aware I was leaving until a few moments ago." He shook Sir Stirling's outstretched hand. "And the lady did not afford me the opportunity to pack."

"Ah. I take it the countess is no longer enamored by your…charms?" Kitted out in Weston's finest black morning suit and a handsome many-caped greatcoat, the man conversed as if encountering a gentleman being cast into the street by a mistress happened on a daily basis. Well, it had happened to Theo more than once. Twice. Very well, this was the fourth time, but would it hurt Sir Stirling to act a bit surprised?

"The problem was she was a bit too enamored of my charms. The woman is insatiable, and I need to be about my work." He glanced at the battered leather satchel at his feet.

"Perhaps you should have informed the lady you were far more interested in her glass house than you were in her bedchamber," Sir Stirling suggested, the tiniest hint of laughter in his tone.

"I will take that under advisement the next time I take on a mistress." Theo plucked his second-best pair of buckskin breeches from the front gate.

"Allow me." Sir Stirling took the breeches and handed them to one of the two footmen behind him.

What the devil?

A handsome travel coach and four, complete with ducal crest, coachman, and outriders, stood before the countess's elegant townhouse. Theo had been so wrapped in his own thoughts and bemoaning Sir Stirling's presence he'd missed its arrival. Or had it been there the entire time? He directed a quick study up and down the street. Not a soul stirred, save for Sir Stirling and his retinue.

Without a word, the footmen moved to gather up Theo's clothes and pack them into the two bags the widowed Countess of Mulhaven had so graciously flung from her bedchamber window. Two pair of Hessians and a stream of colorful language wafted over the sill. Countess or not, Malvina had the vocabulary of a Seven Dials cock-bawd. The duke's servants were efficient and quiet as the grave. Better yet, they had a reputation for their loyalty and discretion. Theo would prefer to keep his humiliation private. Every newspaper and gossip rag in Edinburgh stood ready to proclaim it otherwise.

"I do appreciate you help," Theo said, as he picked up his satchel.

"No, you don't, Grindon. Your stubborn pride is what landed you in this state." Sir Stirling took his arm and guided him toward the coach. "But you will."

Theo planted his feet and turned back to the house. "I must retrieve my plants and my books. God only knows what Malvina will do once she remembers—"

"I suspect even the Almighty shudders at what the countess will do should you venture back into that house." Sir Stirling retrieved a calling card and a sealed note from the inside pocket of his finely tailored morning jacket. "Robert will arrange to retrieve your plants and books and send them along to Hampstead after us." He handed the note and card to one of the footmen. The servant bowed and strode to the front door of Number 14.

"Hampstead?" Theo continued to look over his shoulder as the Scotsman—surprisingly strong for a man his size—dragged him to the coach and shoved him, satchel and all, into the opulent blue velvet seat behind the coachman. "Why the devil would I want to go all the way to Hampstead?" The coach sprang into motion, nearly throwing him to the floor.

"Because you have been given your *congé* by every widow in Scotland with a glass house or conservatory large enough to tempt you." Sir Stirling opened a convenient door inset beneath one of the coach windows and extracted a small decanter and two glasses. "My lady wife describes you as an imminent scandal in search of a place to launch itself."

"Her Grace is too kind." Theo downed the glass of brandy Sir Stirling handed him.

"Her Grace knew the countess was done with you long before this morning's performance. Did you think I appeared in Charlotte Square at dawn by accident?"

Theo glanced out the coach window and ascertained they indeed were traveling out of Edinburgh—and none too slowly, at that. "I would not presume to know why you do anything. As for your lady wife…"

"Take care," Sir Stirling murmured as he gave his fingernails a feigned perusal.

"She is reputed to be a most obliging and attentive listener. And God knows the Countess Mulhaven loves to talk."

"Precisely why we are on our way to Hampstead." Sir Stirling retrieved a packet of documents from a thin leather portfolio on the seat next to him. "By this evening, half of Edinburgh will think you the most heartless rake in Scotland."

"And the other half?" Theo folded his arms across his chest and stiffened his posture to fight against the swaying of the coach.

"Will think you have made a lucky escape. I have a proposition for you, Grindon. One that will secure you a permanent abode and a glass house certain to make even a stout-hearted Sassenach like you swoon."

Theo snorted and stretched his legs across the coach, angling his body to accommodate their length. "I have never swooned in my life. What is your proposition, and why do I have to flee to Hampstead to take it up?"

Sir Stirling handed him the documents. With a put-upon sigh, Theo unfolded the pages and began to read. The early hour and his habitual lack of sleep must have muddled his head. Nothing else accounted for the contents of the neatly penned pages. He quickly scanned the first three pages again.

"These are marriage settlements." Theo flung the papers at the duke as if they carried some virulent plague.

"So they are." Sir Stirling caught and carefully folded them. "You need a place to live and work. I know of a lady in need of a husband."

"You are completely out of—"

"It is you, my friend, who is out. Out of choices, out of money, and out of places where you have not left a trail of murder-minded ladies. This is the perfect solution."

"Since when is marriage the perfect solution for anything?" The walls of the carriage began to close in on him. Theo feared he'd rather leap from a moving coach than be leg-shackled to some woman for the rest of his life.

"When it involves a lady with no interest in your charms or in interfering with your work. She needs a husband to ensure she retains her home and her fortune. You need a home and a place in which to conduct your experiments and raise your plants without the added burden of a wife who wishes to live in your pocket. It is the perfect arrangement."

"In Hampstead." Theo lowered his folded arms and dug his fingers into the plump, velvet seat cushion. "Why does the lady not wait for the Season to commence and acquire a husband in London? Why send you to kidnap an obscure botanist with no title or money to his name?"

"The lady is in desperate need of obscurity. More to the point, she is in need of a husband who is blameless, dull, unknown by London Society and—so far as all good *ton* is concerned—bathed in obscurity," Sir Stirling explained, his face a mask of utter boredom.

The faint toll of a warning sounded in the back of Theo's mind. "I thought I was a scandal in search of—"

"In Edinburgh, yes. Hence your need to remove to the land of your birth."

"You make me sound like an army sounding retreat."

"Should your past mistresses put their heads together, you may well end up a casualty of war. There are times when a hasty retreat is the best move a man can make. A marriage between yourself and Miss Turner is the perfect arrangement for both of you."

"Miss Turner?" Theo held out his glass for Sir Stirling to refill.

"Miss Eden Turner. She is her late father's sole heir, but there are certain…legal issues which necessitate she marry in order to vouchsafe her property and fortune from those who may seek to relieve her of her rightful inheritance."

Theo sipped his brandy and allowed his mind to turn over the morning's events and possibilities. The coach rolled on at a smart pace. The last vestiges of the city disappeared from view. Scenes of the countryside in the direction of the Great North Road slipped by the windows. Much as Theo's life had done over the past ten years.

The Scots duke knew him far better than he'd have credited. As great an anathema as he found marriage, the idea of a permanent place to pursue his work and lay his head had its appeal. He'd drifted through life thus far with only botany as his anchor. Drifting into such a marriage as Sir Stirling described was no worse. Especially if it came with a sizeable glass house and a disinterested wife. Still, something did not ring true about this proposition. The nervous tap of warning at the back of his neck had grown more forceful with every mile they traveled. It always did when something was too damned good to be true.

"Her father is dead, you say?"

Tap-tap-tap.

"These three months."

Tap-tap-tap.

"She would marry before she puts off her blacks?"

Tap-tap-tap.

"She must."

Tap-tap-tap.

"She knows of my past…indiscretions?"

Miss. Eden. Turner.

"She does."

Turner. He knew that name.

"And she is not scandalized?"

Where had he heard that name?

"Let us say, the lady is well-acquainted with scandal, though not of her own making."

Turner.

"Who is her father?" Theo waited for confirmation of his nascent suspicions.

"The man is dead." Sir Stirling's reticence did not bode well, even for someone who'd led as ramshackle a life as Theo.

"What was his name?"

"Dr. James Turner."

Theo sat up slowly. The empty glass slipped from his nerveless fingers to the coach floor. "Dr. James Turner? Care to tell me, *Your Grace,* how marriage to the daughter of

England's most notorious murderer will improve my situation?"

St. George wept again. One could hardly blame him. The urge to weep often came over Eden Turner when her housekeeper, Mrs. Styles, was on a tear. England's sainted dragon slayer, at least the one adorning the floor to ceiling stained glass window at the far end of the gallery, only wept when it rained. As it was doing now. Eden had so stifled her tears over the past three months, she doubted herself capable of ever shedding one again. A daunting prospect when one had attained a mere twenty-five years of life.

"A botanist," Mrs. Styles railed, for at least the twentieth time since breakfast. "A common Scots botanist."

Eden swallowed a sigh and waited for it to go down. "The gentleman was born and raised in Suffolk."

"With not an honor to his name." The round, stout woman vented her ill temper on the hapless embroidered cushions on the blue and yellow damask chaise longue beneath a portrait of one of Eden's ancient ancestors. Once she'd pounded them into submission, the housekeeper rushed to catch up with Eden, who'd begun the trek back up the gallery to the main house.

"He was knighted by King George for services to the Crown," Eden said.

"And not a feather to fly with."

"I have more than enough money for both of us, provided I am married before anyone discovers—"

"Hush!" Mrs. Styles waddled down the series of Persian carpets as quickly as her short legs permitted and pulled the doors at the end of the gallery closed. "You don't want your troubles to make a meal for every table in Hampstead."

"I have no cause to doubt the loyalty of a soul in this

house and neither do you," Eden said as she reached around Mrs. Styles, opened the doors, and strode down the west corridor to the green drawing room. "It's in everyone's best interest to keep my secrets, and well they know it."

Eden, ever practical, attributed the servants' silence to their attachment to their positions and their fealty to her late father. She'd heard their comments at their meals in the servants' hall and upon her entrance into rooms before silence stole their voices and set their limbs into industrious frenzy.

"A cold one is she, Miss Eden."

"Odd enough, to be sure."

"Naught like her father, God rest his soul."

"And what of this husband Sir Stirling is fetching you from Edinburgh?" Mrs. Styles inquired as she stuffed her faded red hair, generously glazed with silver, back into her cap. "How much does he know? How will we know if we can trust him?"

"You make him sound like a bolt of fabric or a haunch of pork." Eden made her way into the largest of Longbow's drawing rooms and collapsed into one of the high-backed green velvet chairs before the nearside hearth. In spite of its immense size, she preferred this drawing room, with its two large fireplaces, dark carved mahogany mantels, and green and gold décor. She had never been fond of small places. Longbow retained much of its Tudor architecture—low ceilings, narrow corridors, and dark paneled rooms that opened one into another. The more expansive the room, the more easily she drew breath when fear and indecision crept over her doorstep.

Eden spent much of her time in the two largest rooms in the house—this drawing room and the library. Of course, the most commodious and expansive part of the country house in which she'd grown up was her father's conservatory and the adjacent work area that had served as his laboratory. She still enjoyed the conservatory for the most part. The work area, however, was a different thing entirely. She had not ventured there these three months. She had no desire to enter it ever again.

"You'd make better use of a bolt of fabric or a haunch of pork than a whey-faced scholar who prefers books to kisses and is dull as ditchwater to boot." Mrs. Styles wedged her body into the chair opposite, and her hands flitted about the tea tray some obliging footman had left in anticipation of Eden's retreat to her favorite lair.

Eden took the cup of tea Mrs. Styles offered and allowed the dark, heady taste and the rich bergamot scent to seep into her soul. Since her father's death, the broad and demanding things of life fought every day to steal her carefully cultivated serenity. That serenity, which the servants saw as coldness, had been her guiding principle since her mother's death almost twenty years ago. The small, everyday things—a cup of perfectly prepared tea or a chapter or two of Miss Austen's latest novel before bed—those were the stalwart guardians that kept the thieves at bay.

"I have no need for kisses or anything more exciting than ditchwater, at the moment," Eden replied. She perused the tea tray and selected one of Mrs. Deeds' elderberry and lemon tarts. Much preferable to kisses from a *whey-faced scholar* or any other man, for that matter.

Mrs. Deeds, Longbow's cook, had been courted, cajoled, and offered every inducement imaginable to take up a position in several of London's most prestigious homes. To the relief of everyone in the household, the whirlwind of a woman had a horror of *Town* and the *murder and mayhem* therein. Hampstead was as close as she cared to set foot. These days, Eden held the same sentiments, though for altogether different reasons.

"What you have need of is a handsome rascal to warm your bed, make you smile, and give you a babe or three. I daresay, this Scots botanist doesn't know one end of a woman from t'other."

Eden nearly choked on her tea. She snatched a serviette from the tray and blotted the bodice of her lavender merino gown. "A handsome rascal is the last thing I need. And you can rest assured, he will not have leave to acquaint himself with either end of my…person, husband or not."

"*Hmph!*" Mrs. Styles hefted herself to her feet and stormed, as much as one might storm whilst swaying side to side like a barrel in a millpond, out of the drawing room toward the entrance hall, muttering all the while, "Has a husband delivered like a roast from the butcher's and doesn't intend to make the one good use of him a man is fit for. And not a whit of courtship to make it worthwhile. It's those novels she reads. Puts strange ideas into a girl's head. I told Dr. Turner…" The rest of her tirade trailed into the entrance hall in the direction of the kitchens.

Novels.

Eden plucked another tart from the delicate Sèvres plate and gave it a savage bite. The only idea Miss Austen's novels had given her was Sir Stirling had better deliver a Mr. Collins and *not* a Mr. Darcy. All her father's friends had deserted them both in the weeks before his death and especially afterwards. With good reason, at least in the eyes of most of Society. Only Sir Stirling James had come to call, listened to her dilemma, and offered a solution. She'd had no choice but to trust him. And she did, to the extent she was able. She'd inherited a house on Charles Street in London, the house and small estate at Longbow, and a considerable fortune—thanks to her father's longstanding and lucrative medical practice as physician to the *ton*'s finest and wealthiest families.

She picked up her cup of tea and went to the front windows overlooking the fading front lawns and yew-lined drive. The plush green velvet cushions of the window seat beckoned. She settled onto the seat, kicked off her slippers, and drew her feet and legs up into the cozy space. How many hours had she spent just so, a book in her hand, waiting for Papa to come home from a call to that countess with a megrim or this viscount with gout or a duke's heir…?

The same profession that had provided them a genteel competence and more had been Papa's downfall. Beset on three sides by threats to her inheritance, Eden was desperate enough and, yes, frightened enough, to entertain Sir Stirling's proposition. She'd had her doubts he'd find a man amenable to marriage under her intended conditions. Then she wondered, what sort of man would agree to such an arrangement?

The answer no longer mattered, so long as he was willing and compliant. Sir Stirling had assured her that a permanent home and access to Papa's immense conservatory were all her bartered bridegroom required. Rather like purchasing a great hulk of a dog or one of the colorful parrots she'd seen for sale on London's docks. Food, water, and an appropriate place to house the creature. As romantic as beef broth, but at least as practical, if not more so. Papa had ingrained lessons on the futility of romance and the safety of the practical into Eden's very bones from the time she was a little girl. No romantic expectations assured one a life without disappointments.

She slipped two fingers into the pocket of her dress. The frightening affirmation of the necessity of her decision to marry crinkled beneath her fingers. The latest had arrived this morning. Disappointments and romantic expectations be damned. Practicality was her only choice.

Eden sipped the last of her tea and stared out the window

at the persistent drizzle, which had settled into the late morning landscape like an old lady's wool shawl. The line of majestic old yews stood sentry on either side of the drive as it emerged to circle the fountain and flowerbeds before the house. From there, the cobblestoned carriageway ducked under the front portico where coaches might disgorge their passengers out of inclement weather. Pity life did not afford one a similar cover from a parent's inclement behavior.

Her teacup empty and her own storms to weather, Eden unfolded her legs and left her comfortable perch. As she turned to place the fragile china on the inlaid table next to the window seat, a flash of motion caught her eye. She blinked a few times to clear her vision. A coach, a behemoth of a traveling coach with outriders before and aft, made its way up the drive at a decorous pace. She did not need to see the coat of arms on the door to know whose conveyance it was. If she had any doubt, the frantic shush of footsteps in the corridor and the deafening slam of the drawing room doors being flung open soon put questions to rest.

"Your haunch of venison has arrived," Mrs. Styles announced, holding her side and huffing between words.

"Mrs. Styles." Those two words, pronounced in the briskly precise tones of Creevy, Eden's high-in-the-instep butler, spoke chapter and verse. Longbow's highest ranked servant was not amused by the housekeeper's pronouncement and was even less amused by her usurpation of his duty to inform the lady of the house of the approach of visitors.

"Thank you, Creevy," Eden said quickly in an effort to halt a squabble between the two before it began. "If you will see to welcoming our guests, I will be there momentarily."

"Of course, Miss." He bowed, directed a bland glare at the housekeeper, and quit the room as quietly as he'd entered.

"Toplofty old blowhard." Mrs. Styles took Eden's arm in a ruthlessly sturdy grip. "You'd think he was the Duke of

Butlers instead of plain-as-a-turnip Roddy Creevy of Cheapside. Come along, Miss."

"Come—" Eden made a valiant attempt to step into her slippers so she could stumble along in her housekeeper's wake. Failing that, she was dragged across the thick, yellow Aubusson like a disobedient hound. "Where am I going?"

"To change out of that ugly dress. Even a bought and paid for bridegroom might have trouble mustering a bit of excitement about a bride dressed like a parson's widow." Mrs. Styles might waddle, but once she worked up a good head of steam, grown men were hard put to balk.

"I don't want him excited," Eden declared as her cold feet slipped on the stone floor of the corridor. "I want him wed and out of my way. Mrs. Styles, stop!" She wrested her arm free and took a moment to catch her breath. Rather than enter the hall from the drawing room, they'd traversed the west corridor and ducked into what had been her father's bedchamber. She glanced about, confused.

"Any woman of sense wants a man wed and out of the way," Mrs. Styles assured her. She opened the door into Papa's private book room and study and waved Eden to join her. "Short of doing him in on the wedding night, there's little chance of that."

At least the bedchamber and study sported carpets and rugs over polished oak floors. Her feet began to thaw a little. And their proximity to the monstrous conservatory, which spanned the length of Longbow, provided a bit of ambient heat.

Eden suddenly realized the point of Mrs. Styles' circuitous route through the house. The housekeeper hoped to secret her into the back of the entrance hall and up the stairs before Creevy ushered their guests out of the October chill.

"I am not changing my dress to meet a mere Scots

botanist." Eden spun on her bare heel and marched out of the book room, through the staircase hall, and into the vestibule with Mrs. Styles hot on her heels. She arrived in time for Creevy to open the double front doors.

Once inside, Sir Stirling James handed the butler his hat and gloves and began to shoulder out of his greatcoat. He stopped, one sleeve off and the other on, to offer Eden a solemn bow.

"Miss Turner."

Sir Stirling's words floated across the entryway as if from far away. She hadn't the ability to acknowledge his bow with a curtsey or any other obeisance due a man of his rank. She was…thunderstruck. To the point, Eden vowed she smelled the scorch of lightning.

Framed in the doorway was the tallest, most brutally handsome man she had ever seen. Hair as black as a starless night framed marble features carved as if by the finest sculptor's hand. Sharp cheekbones, a blade of a nose, a stubbornly squared chin—all highlighted to perfection eyes the green of Longbow's darkest yews and a mouth both serious and sensual at once.

Oh! No, no, no!

Eden stormed across the entrance hall, startling both her butler and her father's friend into stepping back. The dark-haired Adonis in the doorway opened his mouth to speak. Eden shut the doors in his face and collapsed against the carved panels as if defending against an invading army. Before she could utter a word, the portly housekeeper bumped her away with a well-directed hip, snatched open one of the doors, grabbed the gentleman by his coat sleeve, and dragged him inside.

"We'll take him," Mrs. Styles declared.

CHAPTER 2

Miss Eden Turner had the prettiest toes Theo had ever seen. Why they peeped up at him from beneath the hem of that most unattractive gown at this moment was as much a mystery to him as the idea he found them…attractive. Then, in a whirl of lavender skirts, those toes disappeared as his prospective bride led him and Sir Stirling into the salon across the entrance hall. He knew it to be the salon when she'd dismissed Theo without a backward glance and began barking orders at her servants with the precision of an artillery sergeant.

"A tray in the salon, Creevy, if you please. Sandwiches, tea, and coffee. Our guests will be in need of sustenance. Mrs. Styles, see that their luggage is delivered to their rooms. Now."

"At once, Miss." The butler evinced a florid gravitas royal dukes might envy. Not to mention the retreating tread of an Irish haint. The housekeeper who had instigated Theo's precipitous entrance into the house, however, was another matter. She offered him a saucy wink and disappeared down a corridor behind the stairs, bellowing for two unfortunates named Charlie and Pip.

"Come along, Grindon." Sir Stirling nudged Theo forward across the Aubusson done in shades of cream, blue, and brown.

Theo rubbed his arm to erase the effects of the house-keeper's grip. Thank God, he'd ducked in service to the low doorway or he'd be sporting a bump on the head, as well.

Their hostess waved a negligent hand at two ivory, gold, and brown brocade-tufted chairs before a tall, cream-colored marble fireplace. She settled onto the middle of the matching love seat opposite them, feet tucked under her skirts and hands folded in her lap.

"Miss Eden Turner," Sir Stirling intoned graciously, "may I make known to you Sir Theophrastus Grindon, lately of Edinburgh. Theo, allow me to introduce you to the mistress of Longbow, Miss Eden Turner."

Theo bowed over the hand she reluctantly offered. "Miss Turner." The scent of *Convallaria majalis*, lily of the valley, radiated faintly from her skin. "Enchanted to make your acquaintance."

She snorted and drew her hand away, shooing him toward a chair. "Enchanted to make the acquaintance of my money and my father's conservatory, if what Sir Stirling has told me is true."

He clenched his jaw and tossed the Scots duke a disparaging glare. When he returned his focus to the sharp-tongued woman he was to marry, he found her studying him, head tilted and eyes narrowed.

"As you say, Miss Turner. Not to put too fine a point on the situation."

Dove grey eyes—framed by thick, dark eyelashes—widened, lending an exotic air of delight to her expression.

Her lips moved as if to speak, but the arrival of tea trays sent ripples across the bated calm that had settled between them.

The austere butler and two young maids made quick and quiet work of arranging a veritable buffet of sandwiches, little cakes, and tarts on the marquetry tea table between the two chairs and love seat. A silver tea service and an equally splendid coffee service remained on their trays, placed onto a folding table drawn before one end of the love seat. The better for Miss Turner to pour for her guests.

Guests.

In the next day or two, Theo was to marry this woman who behaved as if entertaining a bridegroom brought down for her from the wilds of Scotland by a ducal marriage maker was an everyday occurrence. He took the cup of tea she offered, and while she prepared a cup for Sir Stirling, studied the daughter of one of England's most scandalous gentlemen.

Eden. She put him in mind of a delicate, emergent garden. She was tall for a woman, though a good six inches shorter than Theo. And slender, with long, graceful limbs and slight hints of curves. Nothing like the buxom, erotically built women he chose. Or did they choose him? No matter. Eden Turner possessed an evocative beauty Theo was hard pressed to define.

Her skin was a combination of porcelain and cream, set off to perfection by heavy blue-black hair piled atop her head and held in place by carved tortoiseshell combs. A natural blush of pink touched her cheekbones, which were some-what sharp for a female face. Her chin was a bit squared yet dainty, and her nose was pert to the point of condescension. Her forehead remained high and expressive when her other features were not. And those odd, soft gray eyes framed by lush, exotic lashes reminded him of the mists drifting across a loch on a winter's morning.

"Sir Theophrastus?"

She'd caught him staring. *Damn!* He took the expensive china plate, replete with selections from the tea table, she offered in her long-fingered hand. His thumb brushed her fingers as he took the Sevres from her. She drew back so sharply that he almost dropped the plate.

"Theo," he finally said, as she served Sir Stirling.

"I beg your pardon?" She'd wrapped her hand around the fingers he'd touched and settled the clasped ball they made into her lap.

"If we are to be married, I'd prefer you use a name that does not take five minutes to pronounce." Theo was hungry and the sandwiches, made of fresh bread, roast beef, and Somerset cheddar, tasted far better than the coaching inn food along the way or the insipid fare served in the Countess of Mulhaven's home. He'd polished off the first sandwich in a few bites and was well into the second when he discovered he'd garnered the undivided attention of both Sir Stirling and Miss Turner. He continued to chew, then paused to wash down the bite with a sip of tea.

"I understand your aversion to the use of your full name, sir," Miss Turner said. "One would hate to take more time than necessary to call you to your dinner."

Sir Stirling, the arse, chuckled behind his teacup.

The lady poured herself a cup of coffee, added two lumps of sugar, and took a long sip. "You told me all he required was a bedchamber and a glass house, Sir Stirling. You failed to inform me the expense of feeding a botanist might necessitate laying in stores equal to those needed to feed one of Wellington's regiments on campaign."

"I am to marry a woman I cannot bed for a fortune I may not touch," Theo replied, his tone and words brusquer than he intended. "I would hope you would not begrudge me a few good meals and a brandy now and then. A man must feed some of his appetites." He dropped the now empty plate onto the tea table. He shrugged a shoulder against the nascent irritation meandering up his spine. Not even an hour in Miss Turner's presence and already she cut up his peace. Theo had no desire to contemplate a lifetime of the same.

"I gain a tenant for life in the bargain. Which of us has made the worst purchase?" With her cup halfway to her lips, Miss Turner smiled. "And I can assure you, food and drink are the only appetites you will be satisfying, Sir *Theo*."

"Happy to hear it, Miss Turner. If you will excuse me?" He stood and turned to his old friend. "Might I speak with you in private?"

Sir Stirling raised an eyebrow but continued to sip his tea. Theo glanced at the mistress of Longbow. A sphinx betrayed more feeling, which tore at something in him. Perhaps the roast beef had turned. With certainty, he would not be marrying—

"Miss Turner, perhaps you might show Sir Theo your father's library and the conservatory." Sir Stirling and the lady rose in tandem. He waved her ahead of him and grabbed Theo's arm to drag him along at some distance behind her. She did not look back but led them out a door at the far end of the salon and down a corridor.

Theo leaned in to whisper at Sir Stirling, "This is impossible. She doesn't want a husband. I'm surprised her butler and footmen are male."

"Your legendary charm must not have made it into your luggage," Sir Stirling replied. "You have set her out of curl in less than six sentences. Something of a record, I should think."

They crossed beneath the grand front staircase and entered a small bedchamber done in shades of burgundy and gold. Theo had to duck once more to avoid the low-set door-frame. He'd already surmised, on this floor, at least, he'd forever be doing so. This portion of the house had been a

Tudor mansion, although on approach the house looked to be more in the Palladian style.

"Your bedchamber," Miss Turner announced. Her eyes pinned Theo like a butterfly on a specimen board. She did not tarry to hear Theo's opinion but continued out a set of doors into the next room.

"That woman was born out of curl," Theo said. He stood in the middle of the snug yet immaculate bedchamber and craned his neck to assure himself they were not overheard. "You must see how utterly unsuitable this situation is."

"When did you lose your courage for a challenge?"

"About the same time as you lost your wits and decided Miss Eden *Termagant* Turner was the wife for me. Never mind the rumors about her father, I—"

"You wanted a wife who had no use for your services in bed," Sir Stirling reminded him.

"I also wanted a bed I might sleep in without having to keep one eye open."

"Afraid she'll toss your drawers out the window whilst you sleep?"

"You're an arse, Your Grace. I'm afraid she'll toss *me* out the window whilst I sleep."

"Gentlemen?" Miss Turner called from the next room.

Sir Stirling gave Theo a gentle shove in the direction of her inquiry. Theo dragged his feet across the Persian carpets. He took two steps into the adjoining room and stopped.

"My father's library," Miss Turner said. Her voice played at boredom, the way a talented but far too weary actress might when acting too long in the same play. Yet her eyes betrayed far more, and he glanced away from her rather than contemplate its meaning.

"Good God," Theo murmured.

The room had undoubtedly been part of the original Tudor house. It stretched long and wide down the length of the ground floor. The floors were flagstone, covered in over-lapping Persian rugs woven in patterns of red, black, and gold. Floor to ceiling bookcases lined the walls. Apparently, the windows on what had once been a walking gallery had been filled in and covered over with rich light oak paneling, which kept a room with only a towering bow window on the far end from being so dark. Two fireplaces, tall enough for Theo to stand in, broke up the line of bookcases along the interior wall.

Theo stepped around Miss Turner and prowled the room, stopping to inspect the few open books on the library tables in the middle. Three ornate book stands beckoned from one end, away from the window. Each contained an open book beneath a glass cover. Theo moved from one to the other, touched his fingers to the glass, and mouthed the titles. A chill of reverence chased up his spine.

THE GRETE HERBAL BY PETER TREVERIS
     Bancke's Herbal by Richard Banckes
     A New Herball by…

"WILLIAM TURNER." THEO TURNED TO FACE THE WOMAN WHO, in every way, was ridiculously unsuited to marry any man, even one who had no intention of being a true husband. "A relative?"

"Indeed. Many of the books in this library were his. My father inherited them." She waved a dismissive hand. "I suppose once we are married, they will be yours and you are welcome to them. I have no use for such things, at all." She strolled toward a gap between the rows of bookcases along the outside wall, and the swishes of her skirt revealed flashes of her bare feet. Theo found he could not look away from those glimpses.

"Some of these books are four hundred years old." He stormed after her. "You have a first edition of Turner's *New Heraball*, all three parts. Are you not fond of books, Miss Turner?" He understood her abhorrence of men, somewhat, but what sort of person had no use for books?

She looked over her shoulder as her hands clasped the handles of a set of tall wooden doors he had not realized were there. "I am inordinately fond of books, sir. So long as they have nothing to do with medicine or anything medicinal in nature. I have an extensive library of my own on the first floor. Where my bedchamber is also located, not that you will be in need of that information. Shall we?" She slid the doors apart, into the walls behind the bookcases.

Theo rolled his eyes and spun on his heel only to slam into his grinning friend. Sir Stirling grabbed Theo's arms and attempted to change his direction. "You came all this way; do you not wish to see the conservatory?"

"The only thing I wish to see is the front door and the North Road." Theo refused to move no matter how forcefully Sir Stirling shoved him. "The library was a clever touch, Your Grace, but not even that can induce me to—"

A wave of damp, hot air struck him between the shoulders. The hairs at the back of his neck stirred. He glanced behind him. A set of French windows, hidden by the sliding wooden doors, stood open. A miasma of scents, sweet and exotic and pungent, slithered into the library and wrapped Theo in a blanket of tropical heat and moisture. Helpless to fight the siren call, he stepped onto a wide mosaic path and followed it between an avenue of *Encephalartos altensteinii*, thick, short palms from Africa.

"This way, Sir Theo."

Not even Miss Turner's impatient command managed to

draw him from the haze of enchantment surrounding him. He followed the colorful path farther into the glass house, Sir Stirling close on his heels. Each panel of the vaulted glass ceiling appeared to be attached to a series of lines and levers. To open and close sections one at the time? The tinkle of running and splashing water lured him into an open circular space. The path split around a large raised pool, out of which rose a towering fountain.

Theo wandered around the fountain and struggled to look everywhere at once. No matter which way he turned his gaze, he saw walls of green and kaleidoscopes of exotic flowers from all over the world. Try as he might, the end of the conservatory eluded him. The width of the room—nay, building—was at least equal to that of the main house, if not more. In the distance, he spied worktables and shelves upon shelves of potted herbs. His head began to swim.

"What do you think, Sir Theo?" a sultry, contralto voice inquired.

He trained his regard in a languid perusal of the direction from which the question had come. He realized who had spoken with an amazed start. On a black brocade chaise longue in an alcove cut into an arch of hibiscus trees in full bloom, Eden Turner sat, her feet tucked beneath her skirts. She stared at him, her head cocked as if she expected him to say something clever or perhaps run for the doors. Heat that had nothing to do with the conservatory shot up his body from the soles of his feet to the top of his head.

"Yes," Sir Stirling spoke behind him. "What do you think?"

"I think you are an unmitigated scoundrel," Theo muttered out of the side of his mouth. "Give me the marriage settlements and find me a quill and ink before I change my mind."

The sphinx in the lavender dress neither blinked nor uttered a word.

. . .

THEO LAY ON THE COMFORTABLY FIRM MATTRESS OF HIS NEW bed, stared at the pleated silk of the bed's canopy supported by thick, carved bedposts, and sighed. He turned on his side for the hundredth time and watched the fire in the grate shimmer with heat. He'd have to work to grow accustomed to the low ceilings in many of the rooms. However, those same overhead, low-paneled expanses ensured the rooms stayed warm against the October nighttime chill. Unfortunately, they did little to warm the chill of the woman he was to marry in less than twelve hours.

Eden.

Now, he truly had no hope of slumber. With a snarl of frustration, he flung aside the covers and threw his legs over the side of the bed. After a few blind tries, he managed to jam his feet into the dancing shoes his first mistress had gifted him. The same shoes she'd shied at his head on his way out the door. He'd had little use for them since, but they served as slippers in a pinch. He retrieved a quilted silk banyan from the foot of the bed, slipped into it, and tied its belt in a savage knot.

With a full belly from a delicious dinner and two glasses of excellent brandy, Theo had hoped to garner a full night's rest before stepping into the parson's mousetrap in the morning. The meal had been sumptuous, and Sir Stirling had been congenial and the soul of entertainment and grace. Miss Turner had shocked him with her knowledge of the goings on in Parliament and her amiable friendship with Sir Stirling.

She'd appeared the consummate hostess, a role she'd no doubt served when her father was alive. She'd also shown an uncanny ability to act as if he were not even there, save for when he interjected himself into the conversation with a pithy remark. During which, she'd pin him with those mist-colored eyes and make him incapable of speech. Instances which Sir Stirling marked with a quarter of a grin or the lift of an eyebrow.

Theo had tried introducing every topic in his considerable repertoire to no avail. Short and sharp replies were his only reward. Eventually, he devoted himself to his food and to a surreptitious study of the lady at the head of the mahogany table centered in the pale green and ivory, Adam-decorated dining room. His study proved fruitless for the most part. He knew no more about her than he'd learned in the first hour of their acquaintance. And tomorrow, he'd be bound to her for the rest of his life.

He made his way into the library. Moonlight from the tall bow window at the far end of the room splashed across the library tables, bookcases, and other furnishings. It took a moment for his eyes to adjust to the dim light. He strode to the sliding doors and let himself into the conservatory, swiftly pulling the French windows closed behind him to keep in the heat.

For several long breaths, he merely stood, eyes closed, and drew in the serenity of Longbow's glass walled piece of heaven. Every good and warm memory of his life was painted against a background of riotous green growth flourishing in places the plants had no right to grow. He'd spent the better part of his childhood learning the mysteries of plants from his father's mother, an avid gardener, and a woman who knew exactly what sort of father her son had become.

His grandmother's conservatory in Suffolk had served as his refuge, his library, his solace against a father to whom he'd always been a disappointment and a mother too devoted to his older brother to spare a moment's defense for her quiet, studious, youngest child. He'd bought his own commission at the age of seventeen to prove his worth to his father, only to return to Suffolk after Waterloo to find he had no father, no family, no home left.

Until now.

By this time tomorrow, he'd be in possession of a home—on paper, at least. More or less. He'd be in possession of a bedchamber, a library, and a conservatory. Considering he'd owned only two portmanteaus of clothing, most fit for the ragman, two days ago, his fortunes had improved considerably. He opened his eyes and set out on one of the mosaic paths he'd not taken on his earlier visit to Longbow's beautiful glass house. Fortunately, a few lit lanterns hung on wrought iron stands in the less foliaged areas. He came to a dense forest of banana trees, pineapple plants, and oddly enough, gardenia bushes. He knelt to examine the roots of the pineapple plants.

"You really must eat, George," a soft, instantly recognizable, contralto voice urged from the other side of the heavy forest. "You have chosen a devilishly inappropriate time to embark on a slimming regime."

Theo tried to peer through the greenery to discover who this mysterious George might be. He, of all people, had no right to expect a lady of five and twenty to have lived like a nun. He did, however, take a modicum of umbrage at the idea of his bride having a lover in the house the night before their wedding. He did have some scruples…a few scruples… very well, one scruple.

She stood beneath the light of one of the lanterns close to the wall of glass facing the back gardens. Her skin glowed beneath a halo of lamplight and moonlight, her hair one long ebony braid against the pale blue wool of her night rail. She put him in mind of—

"It's a pity you cannot borrow a bit of appetite from the

Scots botanist Sir Stirling brought me. He certainly has appetite to spare."

What the devil! Theo half stood and then thought better of it.

"If marrying a man who eats like one of those hairy Highland coos is the price of our security, it is a price I will have to pay, George. I'll not take a chance on losing our home and fortune to the thieves I've been fending off since Papa… left us."

Theo fell back on his arse. What had Sir Stirling I-know-what's-best James landed him in this time? He'd fended off the advances of amorous women since he was thirteen. No one said anything about fending off thieves. Perhaps he should—

"He is far too handsome and charming for his own good."

Theo leaned back on the surprisingly warm path and propped himself on his elbows. He fought a self-satisfied grin. From where he lay in the shadows, he had a clear view of Longbow's termagant angel, as he'd come to think of her.

"Until he opens his mouth to speak," she mused, and looked back over her shoulder at the mysterious George, Theo assumed. "In my favor, he seems prone to nattering on, which ensures I shall be perfectly safe."

Theo dropped his chin to his chest.

"I suggest you find your bed, Sir Theo. It will not do for a man who trades on his handsome face to look haggard on his wedding day. Unless you intend to find Sir Stirling and cry craven again? Come along, George."

Theo scrambled to his feet in time to see a slip of pale blue disappear into the darkness toward the far end of the conservatory. He raced along the mosaiced path in that direction only to find an embroidered silk handkerchief at the base of a trellised wall woven with vines of *Wisteria floribunda* and *Wisteria sinensis*. Nothing more. He snatched it up and made to stuff it in the pocket of his banyan. Unable to stop himself, he lifted it to his nose to inhale the scent of lily of the valley.

"Good night, Sir Theo," drifted out of the darkness.

He turned only to see those portions of the conservatory touched by the changeable paths of winking moonbeams and flickering lamplight. Where the hell had she gone so quickly? What strange magic worked in the willowy hellion who ruled over Longbow? And who the devil was George?

CHAPTER 3

"I MUST SAY"—EDEN TURNED FROM THE DRAWING ROOM window overlooking the portico—"that was a perfectly good waste of a new dress." She smoothed her hands down the silvery gray silk skirts of the gown she'd worn to become Lady Grindon a little over an hour past.

"A waste?" Mrs. Styles handed her a cup filled with coffee, curls of heat rising from it in enticing little puffs of rich decadence. "The poor man was struck dumb the moment he saw you. He'll not be forgetting he has a wife anytime soon. And he won't be allowing you to forget you have a husband either, mark my words."

"He was most definitely struck dumb," Eden mused. She sipped her coffee and gave her attention to the two gentlemen standing next to Sir Stirling's traveling coach. "He's said less than a dozen words to me all morning, including his wedding vows."

"Those are the ones that count. No need to complain, my lady. It takes most wives months to convince a husband to keep his mouth shut." The housekeeper joined Eden at the window. "He'll come 'round."

"That is none of my concern. He said no more than two words to me at the briefest wedding breakfast it has ever been my misfortune to attend. Yet, he has stood out in the cold longer than the wedding and breakfast together taking his leave of Sir Stirling."

Mrs. Styles peered out the window. "Once His Grace leaves, he'll be here all alone with you. P'raps he's afraid." A wicked grin creased her aging cherub's face.

"Afraid?" Eden watched Sir Stirling climb into the coach, gaze up at her thoughtfully, and offer her a brisk wave. She waved back and smiled. The moment her new husband caught her, she dropped her hand and marched across the drawing room to deposit her now empty cup on the tea table. "The man stands half a foot over six feet and weighs a good fifteen stone. What could he possibly have to fear from me?"

"From the way he looked at you when you came down the stairs in that dress"— Mrs. Styles retrieved the tray and cup from the tea table— "everything." Her annoying bray of laughter followed the housekeeper out of the drawing room and down the east corridor toward the kitchens.

The thud of Sir Theo's bootheels heading from the entrance hall toward his bedchamber turned Eden's own steps down the west corridor and into the downstairs library. His library now, too. It rankled, and she had no idea why. A great deal about her newly acquired husband irritated, annoyed, and frankly infuriated her.

He *had* appeared dumbfounded as she'd descended the stairs on Sir Stirling's arm. She'd sensed his eyes on her as he followed them into the salon where the vicar who had ridden up from London with the special license waited to perform the brief marriage ceremony. Sir Theo had recited his vows in a firm, low voice—his gaze never leaving Eden's face, not even when he'd placed the heavy gold band on her finger.

Eden didn't remember her own vows. What woman

would, standing next to a man wearing a dark green morning coat stretched taut by broad muscled shoulders, a white linen shirt, and a neatly tied cravat, with tan buckskins that fit his powerful legs like a second skin? She had to admit —Sir Theo Grindon having just arrived after traveling all the way from Edinburgh by coach was a handsome man. Sir Theo Grindon in new clothes after a night's rest, a bath, and the attentions of Charlie, the footman, was wicked dream inducing. Which also accounted for her making three attempts before she managed to sign the registry the clergyman had brought with him.

Voices and a small commotion from the direction of the conservatory startled her from her schoolgirl mooning—which was what she'd been doing. She needed a good shake and a slap. However, as it was beneath Creevy's dignity and as Mrs. Styles would enjoy it too much, Eden had simply to remember why she'd married in the first place. And how much she had to lose should she become enamored of her husband, let alone trust him. A cold weight settled back upon her shoulders. Not such a bother except that Sir Stirling's assurances and Sir Theo's biting practicality had lifted the weight for a while.

"You lads drop any of these fancy boxes and I 'spect the new master will have all our heads. Take them over to Doctor Turner's work benches. Careful now."

What was Mr. Jobs doing in the conservatory? Eden hurried to the French windows and stepped into Longbow's glass house and into utter chaos. Mr. Jobs, her estate steward, and what might well be the entire stable staff, and a good number of the home farm workers, had formed a line from the exterior French windows at the far side of the room back through the conservatory and deep into what had been her father's work area. They passed crates one to another, as one might pass buckets during the act of dousing a fire. Some of the crates were sealed. Others contained a veritable garden of strange plants and shrubs climbing over the sides as if to escape. Some she knew on sight. Others defied her knowledge of botany.

"Morning, Miss." Mr. Jobs snatched his hat from his head. "Beg your pardon, my lady. The lads and I wish you very happy." All work ceased as the line of men doffed their caps and delivered a series of bows.

"Thank you." Eden managed a twist of a painful smile. "Please carry on whilst I speak with Mr. Jobs." She beckoned her steward and followed the bright blue mosaic path along the wall the library shared with the conservatory. A series of trellises, replete with her mother's climbing roses, hid the brickwork and perpetuated the illusion of a heavenly garden.

"What are all those boxes and plants?" Eden asked once they were out of hearing of the others. "And when did they arrive?"

"They arrived just after sunrise this morning," an amused voice answered from behind her.

Eden turned.

"And they are the sum total of my earthly possessions, Lady Grindon. Thank you, Jobs. That will be all." Her *husband* addressed his last words to the steward but continued to regard Eden with an enigmatic smile playing about his lips.

To his credit, the man who had run Longbow since before Eden's birth looked to her and waited for her terse nod before he took his leave. Sir Theo, the fiend, only raised an eyebrow and winged his arm at her once Jobs disappeared in the direction of the low voices of his workers.

"You brought all this from Edinburgh?" A foolish question, but she had to start somewhere.

"Sir Stirling had it brought. His head footman had the

misfortune of wresting my books and plants from the clutches of…my previous landlady."

"You mean your latest mistress?" Eden allowed him to lead her to the workbenches and shelves at the back of the conservatory. To her ridiculous delight, his cheeks flushed a deep red, but only for a moment.

"I see my old friend was quite the font of information."

"Sir Stirling is a gentleman. He was appropriately vague. His wife, however, was not so reticent."

"I can imagine."

"Needs must, Sir Theo, when the devil takes the reins," Eden said with a shrug. "We all do what we must to survive."

"Has he taken the reins often in your life, *Eden*?"

She stopped and pulled her arm free only to have him clasp her hand. "I…have not given you leave to—"

"It was implied in the wedding vows," he assured her, his tone and expression an attempt at solemnity.

"I don't remember that part."

"Little wonder, as swiftly as you raced through them. I'm not certain the vicar made out every word, but I distinctly remember the word *obey*."

"Of course, you did." Eden tugged her hand from his. A tingling heat raced up her arm and sent her heartbeat into an uneven country dance. She pressed her palm to her middle and stepped away, closer to the work benches, potting tables, and shelves of laboratory equipment. "This is a business arrangement, *Sir Theo*. A mutually profitable contract between two people who entered into it with full knowledge of what to expect."

Liar flashed across the back of her mind. She'd not expected him to be so handsome, so vital, so male. She'd not expected something in him to call to the one thing in her she could not hammer into submission. Loneliness.

Eden closed her eyes and slammed her hand onto the

closest table. A familiar yet unpleasant scent— part of a more unpleasant memory—drew her attention to the plants that now lined the worn wooden surface next to her hand.

"What does the nature of our marriage have to do with the way we address one another?" He reached her in one long stride. "I address many of my business associates by their Christian names."

"Business associates? Is that what they call a man's mistresses in Edinburgh?" Eden drew in a knife-sharp breath and lifted her head to stare into his face. The sly smile she'd pasted upon her lips ached. She dug her nails into the scarred wood of the table. The familiar scent still assailed her but faded to a mere distraction the moment his eyes met hers.

"I do beg your pardon, Lady Grindon," he said in a voice devoid of inflection. "You and I are indeed not business associates. You are my employer. I will not forget myself again. If you will excuse me, I must see to the arrangement of my experiments." He took up her free hand, bowed over it, and made a purposeful retreat to the stack of crates at the back of the work area.

She watched him go about emptying crates and ordering the placement of pot after pot of seedlings. She'd hurt him. Eden would take her oath on it. Which had been her intention. Which was always her intention. She'd simply believed a man who'd lived a cavalier life to be incapable of hurt. Just as the world saw her as impervious to the sideways glances, the drawn aside skirts, the whispers. Why wouldn't she be? When one had lived on the amorphous line between good Society and the working gentry one's entire life, a stoic acceptance of snubs was to be expected. Should one be so foolish as to step over the line, the reprisals would be swift, severe, and more painful than ever imagined.

Such mawkish musings aided nothing and no one. She turned to leave so quickly she bumped into the footman, Pip, his arms laden with one of the open crates. That familiar scent took her breath away. *Foxglove.* The botanist had brought foxglove into her home. Eden was about to hurt more than his feelings.

"Sir Theo, what is this?" She stormed toward him, one hand curled around the lip of the crate, thereby dragging poor Pip along behind her. Her march halted only when she stood toe to toe with her new husband. He had the audacity to lift one of the plants from the box, inspect it carefully, and place it on the workbench before he tugged his forelock like a common stable boy.

"This one is *Digitalis purpurea,* my lady. Commonly known as foxglove. I should think a physician's daughter would have an acquaintance with—"

"I am well-acquainted with the properties of foxglove," she said, poking the forefinger of her free hand into Sir Theo's hard-as-granite chest with each word. "Which is why I will not have it in my house."

He wrapped his fist around her finger and pressed his fist over his heart. He leaned down so his forehead nearly touched hers and spoke so only she might hear. "It isn't in *your* house. It is in *my* conservatory, which is under *my* dominion according to *our* contract."

His eyes had flecks of gold within the dark green. His breath smelled of the cake Mrs. Deeds had created to serve at the wedding breakfast—all almonds and sugar from the icing, and oranges and hazelnuts and spices from the cake. His grip on her finger was warm and gentle. His skin smelled of sandalwood and something herbal, earthy. She'd erred in drawing this close. From far too early an age, Eden had learned to sense the dangers in people, characteristics hiding or running just beneath the surface. Characteristics others might simply consider the price of being human. At times, her stubborn pride far outlasted her common sense.

"Nevertheless, I must insist you remove it. It is dangerous. I will not be responsible for"—she swallowed to remove the breathless note from her voice--"for any accidents."

With a delicacy she'd never have imagined in a man his size, he slowly opened his fist and smoothed her hand with his fingertips. "There will be no accidents. I will secure the plants. I have spoken with both Creevy and Jobs. No one is to touch anything on any of the workbenches or potting tables. They have both assured me every man, woman, and child in your service is obedient and loyal to a fault." He clicked his heels, bowed, and dropped her hand. "One can hardly blame them," he added with a piercing look before going back to unpacking his crates.

Eden picked up her skirts and walked at as dignified a pace as she was capable, out of the conservatory, through *his* library, up the stairs, and into her own robin's egg blue and buttery yellow library. Her sanctuary. Unfortunately, a botanist with green eyes and a wit entirely too quick to be borne had blown any chance of sanctuary to the devil. She'd started out with Sir Theo the way she had intended to go on and he'd rolled her up foot, horse, and guns. Then he'd insulted her, attributing her servants' good conduct to fear rather than… She dropped into the over-stuffed chintz chair. The rosewood reading table rocked and nearly spilled its small stack of leather-bound novels onto the floor.

What did a man like him know of her life? Her father had demanded a home to which he might invite his aristocratic patients, even when he knew they'd never come. He'd demanded she have a Season, and garnered invitations for her from his titled patrons that they did not want to issue. When her Season had all came to naught, he'd not bothered to discover why, nor had he ever blamed her. In words, at least. She knew. Every day and in every way, he implied his disappointment. She'd failed after he'd depended upon her marrying well to improve their position in Society. And the results led to his death and now to her forced marriage with a...a...

"Ugh!" Eden flounced from her chair and went to the tantalus centered between two of the windows overlooking the front gardens. She lifted the lid of the stand globe and snatched up a leaded glass and a bottle of sherry. After pouring herself a generous portion, she emptied it in one draught and poured a half glass more. Her slippers, as new as the dress, began to pinch. She returned to her chair, put her sherry on the reading table, and reached beneath her skirts to untie the ribbons of the lovely but irritating footwear. After she toed them off, she picked them up and shied them across the room.

Childish? Yes.

Satisfying? Without a doubt.

She would have done better to have waited. Perhaps with more time, Sir Stirling might have found a man with a modicum of gentlemanly manners rather than an effulgence of gentlemanly arrogance and male...virility. Eden groaned and covered her face with her hands. She'd had no more time, not truly.

She had to live in the same house with Sir Theo Grindon, but she did not have to tolerate his rude behavior with either her presence or her attentions. Longbow was not a grand house, nor were the grounds and home farm as vast as other estates farther from London. Longbow was, however, of sufficient size that she and her bartered husband might rub along quite well so long as she spent as little time in his company as possible. She had her own life to lead.

Eden downed the remainder of her sherry in one decidedly unladylike gulp. She'd start by divesting herself of her ridiculous wedding finery. Trouble was that the dress closed with a series of buttons up the back. She twisted, turned, and stumbled her way out of the library and through her little study, clawing at the pugnacious carved bone fasteners with every step.

Several surrendered with a sharp ping as they hit the floor. By the time she reached her private sitting room, enough had given way either by her slipping them free of the buttonholes or tearing them off the dress, she was able to wrench it over her head. She rolled it into a ball, stormed to the window seat, and stuffed it into the little storage cupboard beneath the cushioned lid. She removed her mother's amethyst parure— necklace, earrings, and bracelet—and placed them on the silver tray atop the cherrywood commode next to the window. Her faded blue flannel dressing gown lay across a tapestry work ottoman before the fire. She shrugged into it and tugged the belt into a loose knot.

Rap! Rap! Rap!

Eden jumped and turned toward her sitting room door.

Mrs. Styles. Had to be. No one else knocked with such imperious demand.

A sudden indignance blazed through her. Eden was mistress of her own house, a married woman. She would no longer countenance such complete disregard for her consequence, in this house, at least. She slapped the handle down and yanked the door open so forcefully it propelled her backwards a few stumbled steps.

"You!" Eden righted herself and stepped into the doorway, blocking, as much as she was able, the large figure of her newly wedded husband. In his shirtsleeves and waistcoat, no less. A smudge of dirt marked the crest of one cheek. "What are you doing here? We agreed you were forbidden from this floor."

His eyes widened. His lips half-pursed, as if he could not decide whether to laugh or snarl. "I came to apologize for—"

"Apology accepted. Now leave." Eden stepped back and attempted to slam the door in his face. He blocked its closure with a hand and shoved it open wide.

His face might have been carved in stone, save for the rhythmic pulse in the line of his jaw. His knuckles were white against the dark wood of the door he gripped. "You are, without a doubt, the most bloody-minded, venal, over-bearing, sharp-tongued wench I have ever had the misfortune to meet. I have no idea why I agreed to Sir Stirling's proposition. He caught me in a weak moment. That much is certain."

Sir Theo released the door and took a step closer. Eden refused to let him cow her, even as he continued to rail. "I am most certainly attics to let, but I actually find you attractive and intriguing and the most unique woman I have met in my life." He threw up his hands. "I came up here to apologize. Something I never do, and to ask if you might take supper with me this evening, although the endeavor is sure to give me indigestion."

Eden folded her arms across her chest and bit her lower lip. Her head swam as if she'd suffered a cold for a week. "Bloody-minded, venal, sharp-tongued?" She unfolded her arms and punched two fingers at his sternum. "Attractive, intriguing, unique? Which is it, Sir Theo? I confess I find myself utterly confused."

"Then holy matrimony is not the only thing in which we are joined, Eden." He drew her into his arms. His embrace was gentle, yet allowed her to savor the strength and power in the muscles and sinews his shirt did not hide. His chest rose and fell against hers. "Tell me no, my termagant wife," he breathed across her lips. "Because for some reason not even the Almighty understands, I want to kiss you." He touched his lips to hers, light as the brush of a feather. "Even if it is only once."

The sensation of sinking into a hot bath suffused Eden the instant Theo's mouth settled gently to hers. His kiss urged without demanding and gave without surrender. His lips slanted over hers, drawing her breath and returning it to her heated and laced with temptation. Unlike any bath she'd ever taken, her temperature only increased the longer he kissed her. She started when he nipped the corner of her lower lip, but she did not draw away. He chuckled and pulled her closer, touching the tip of his tongue to the dip of her top lip.

She braced her hands on his biceps and slowly ran her hands up until they splayed in the thick, silky hair at the back of his head.

He groaned and kissed her more deeply.

Eden could not breathe, nor did she want to. She leaned into him, her breasts heavy and sensitive as they rested against his chest. He cradled her face in his hands and turned her head to kiss a trail of hot and tender kisses along her jawline, across her cheek, her nose and onto her other cheek before returning to her mouth. She wanted him to go on forever. She'd settle for a moment more. Two moments. Five. Who knew a man with a chest like a rock might have lips as soft as rose petals?

Rose petals?

She'd run mad. She must stop him. She must—

"Eden," he murmured against her lips.

Oh no!

She raised her hands and stumbled back. Theo caught her elbows to steady her.

"I am fine," she said, only a little breathless. "You may release me now."

He did so, slowly and with great care. "About supper..." He blinked several times and took a deep breath.

"I think not." The words came out in a rush. "You have

your things to unpack and your work to begin." She forced herself to turn and walk to the fireplace. When she faced him once more, the distance helped her to gather her thoughts, as the closer she stood to him the more befuddled they became. "In fact, I would prefer any further invitations or communication between us be conducted by way of the servants."

"The servants?" He narrowed his eyes and cocked his head.

"Yes." She rested her hand on the mahogany mantelpiece. "Communicate your requests and questions to one of the servants, and they can relay them to me. As I will convey my answers to you through them."

"Rather an odd way for husband and wife to communicate, would you not say? What of our more intimate messages? Are we to speak those through servants, as well?" The air smoldered between them, conveyed on the fiery green flare in his eyes.

"I see no reason for us to have anything *intimate* to say to each other." Eden pressed the smooth wood beneath her fingertips. "However, to save our sensibilities, I suggest we write notes."

"Notes?" He appeared genuinely confused.

"Short messages on pieces of paper? I find them to be most efficacious when I wish to express my specific wishes to servants and tradesmen." Her heart thundered so that she marveled he did not see.

He stared at her. A slow smile seeped over his face. Then he laughed, a low, dark sound that tingled deep in her belly and became a shiver over every inch of skin.

"Servants and tradesmen." He fixed her with a gaze devoid of any discernible feeling. "I will not ask which I am. It may well be more lowering than I can bear to hear. But I will not trouble you with my presence again. Good day, madam." With a brief snap of a bow, he turned and quit the room. The *slam* of the door echoed over and over until only a vast, empty silence remained.

A rushing noise came to her ears, as if from a great distance, and then closer. Eden raised her hand shakily to her chest. Its rapid rise and fall shocked her. Her legs turned to jelly. She sank onto the ottoman. The noise was her own ragged breathing. When she clapped her hand to her mouth, she flinched slightly at the tenderness of her lips. A sharp, wet stinging ensued. *Wet?* Salty and wet. Eden rubbed her cheeks with her fists.

"You ridiculous girl," she muttered. "Girl? Those days are long past. You ridiculous woman. Why are you crying?" All the while, the sensation of his lips on hers ran over and over in her mind, like a dream one had and hoped to have again.

She told him to write her notes. Notes, as if he were some lackey and not her husband. Notes.

She stared at the ornate writing desk before the window and at the series of little drawers rising across the back of it. The key to those drawers lay safely tucked into the back of the mantel clock ticking in counterpoint to the rhythm of Eden's breathing.

Why would she ask for more notes, when the ones she'd received since her father's death were the very reason she'd landed with a husband who kissed like Theo Grindon in the first place?

CHAPTER 4

THEO STARED AT THE FOLDED SQUARE OF FOOLSCAP IN THE middle of the silver salver and bit back a sigh. He glanced up at Longbow's long-suffering butler. Creevy's fixed expression of servile boredom indicated nothing as to the contents of this particular missive from Theo's wife of the last fortnight. The poor man's current duties consisted of courier between the mistress of the house and…hell, Theo had no idea of his own position. Definitely not master. He placed the *Hordeum vulgare* plant back into the pot from which he'd removed it to study its roots, dusted off his hands, and took up the note.

Sir,

It has come to my attention the downstairs maids have had to scrub your muddy boot prints out of the salon carpets three times in two days. Might I suggest you don slippers before you enter the main *house? Mrs. Styles can little afford to assign a pair of maids simply to clean up after you all day.*

Lady G

HE CRUMPLED THE NOTE INTO A BALL. CREEVY CLEARED HIS throat—if one might call a brief, pointed *Ahem!* as clearing anything. Theo fumbled on the shelf above his worktable and found a sharpened quill. His search beneath the stacks of papers and journals strewn about the wooden surface proved less fruitful. Creevy, salver still level in one hand, reached around Theo and drew the inkwell from behind a series of potted barley plants. He placed it on the worktable next to the quill. Theo unfurled the note and attempted to smooth the wrinkles from it.

Theo was eighteen when he'd finished at Oxford. Since then, he'd become one of the most respected botanists in England, perhaps all of Britain. He'd also had four mistresses. One before he joined the cavalry at twenty, and three since he'd left the cavalry two years ago, shortly after Waterloo. He'd traded on his handsome face and feigned charm, and subsequently retreated back into his work when the sudden bloom of passion faded, as it always did. Eden Turner had knocked him off his pins in a way no other woman had. His shoulders twitched at the mere thought of her.

Quill poised over the crinkled paper, Theo composed his response, with an eye to provoking the same annoyance in his lady wife as she did in him. Though he doubted Napoleon himself capable of provoking Eden Turner Grindon.

MADAM,

. . .

I SHALL OFFER MY APOLOGIES TO THE MAIDS FOR THE UNDUE WORK I have caused them. As I do not own slippers, I shall not be able to comply with that portion of your edict. However, as going about in one's naked feet is acceptable behavior by the lady of the house, I shall henceforth remove my boots and stockings before leaving the conservatory.

I remain your obedient servant,

SIR T

HE DID NOT TROUBLE HIMSELF TO SAND THE NOTE BUT BLEW on it as he pinched it between thumb and forefinger. Which provided the added bonus of garnering a raised eyebrow from Creevy. Petty, no doubt. Childish, too. Theo's days were his own at Longbow. More than they had been at any other time in his life. His father, his professors at Oxford, those officers over him in the cavalry, his mistresses—they'd all controlled some or all aspects of the way he'd spent his waking hours. The past fortnight had been the most free and productive since his days at Grindon Place as a child, racing his pony across the fields and fishing in the lake. He'd allowed others to rule his life for reasons he had no care to examine. Now, he desired only peace and dominion over his life. He had it.

Save for one inexplicable, maddening, ghastly, damned plague on his thoughts at least one hundred times a day.

"Lady Grindon?"

Theo started. Creevy stared at him, the salver perfectly level, and pointed with his free hand at the note. The note Theo had apparently been waving about like a flag of surrender for the last five minutes. He folded it and tossed it onto the infernal tray.

"By all means, take it to Lady Grindon. Perhaps it will be the only one today." He retrieved another potted barley plant from the shelf.

The butler bowed and turned to walk away.

"And perhaps pigs will fly over Apsley House," Theo muttered, as he loosened the soil in the pot.

"I beg your pardon, sir?" Creevy inquired over his shoulder.

"Could you ask Mrs. Deeds to send a tray with several of her excellent ham sandwiches from the kitchens?"

"Very good, sir." The man disappeared into the foliage like smoke.

Theo returned to his study of the barley plant's roots. He dragged a splotched copy book closer, scattering loose soil across the pages and onto the gray and black cobblestoned floor. The bright mosaics ended where the work area began. Appropriate. Practical. He allowed his gaze to rove to the intricate, colorful tilework that meandered through the lush vegetation—a rainbow's shimmering reflection on a highland loch.

He scrubbed his hands over his face with a feral growl. *Ridiculous.*

A veritable army of antlike stings scampered down the back of his neck. The air rising from the heated floors of the conservatory carried a sudden scent of lily of the valley. Instinctually, he turned toward the French doors, but they remained closed. The system of boilers and pipes beneath the conservatory had at first intrigued and delighted him. Over the past few days, however, the warmth had come to annoy him. Lily of the valley annoyed him.

The quill he'd taken up fell from his hand, spattering ink on his notes. He rose from the stool before the worktable and went to the bank of cupboards set into the farthest recessed wall of the conservatory. As he rummaged for foolscap or some other paper on which to finish his notes, his mind returned to the source of his unwanted, mystifying lack of concentration.

He'd kissed her.

Theo had kissed plenty of women since he'd stolen his first one from the vicar's daughter behind the tomb of some Norman knight in the village church. Most he'd kissed because he had wanted to or needed to in order to seduce them. Of late, he'd learned to kiss from necessity and to feign something he had not felt in years. Passion. Having to kiss for one's supper took a great deal of the charm out of the endeavor. However, it also made the activity safe and easy to dismiss. All the better for his work.

He'd kissed Eden Turner.

He'd kissed his wife.

And he could not stop thinking about it. Dammit. When he least expected it, the taste of her lips burned his. Lily of the valley assailed him all over the house. A pause in his work invited an invasion of heat, soft skin, and the sweet misery of a single kiss he could not drive from his memory. She haunted his dreams at night and awakened him at dawn with a cock stand on which he'd have no trouble hanging his great coat. All from a single kiss. Which she had dismissed as simply as one dismissed a few drops of rain or a cup of tea gone cold.

You are a complete and utter fool, Theo Grindon. Hoisted on your own petard.

He opened and shut cupboard after cupboard in search of something, anything, on which to write. There were empty journals and copybooks in the trunk in his bedchamber. Fetching them, however, necessitated he remove his boots. Shrew of a woman. His first real lust since long before

Waterloo wasted on a cold-hearted, sharp-tongued managing wench who had the power to whither a man's… ardor with a word. And stir it roaring back to life with a mere glance.

Theo conducted an exhaustive search of the last cupboard and stood, fists on hips, shaking his head.

"Put the lady from your mind, Theophrastus," he muttered. "She has banished you to the ground floor and a snowstorm of notes for kissing her. If you do anything else, you'll be sleeping in the stables with the rest of the horseflesh under a veritable forest of missives." He began to toe off his boots when his gaze fell on a dark rosewood chiffonier tucked into an alcove to the side of the bank of cupboards. It appeared bare, save for a thin cover of dust atop it.

Theo jammed his foot back into his boot and limped over to open the doors across the front of the chiffonier. *Journals?* Leather bound journals, some cracked with age and replete with yellowing pages, filled the confines of the interior of the rosewood piece. He set to work dragging each one out and stacking it atop the chiffonier. Once he'd transported them to his worktable, he began to arrange them by date. The pages were filled with research—medical research—written in the same precise hand.

One of Longbow's efficient and too-damned quiet retainers had deposited Mrs. Deeds' response to his request for sandwiches next to his unfinished notes. He poured a cup of tea, took up one of the bread, cheese, and ham master-pieces, and dropped onto the stool to read the journals of the late Dr. James Turner, by an odd twist of fate, his father-in-law. The man all of London had labelled "murderer."

Theo jerked awake. Darkness had fallen. The stars shone above the conservatory's glass ceiling, more visible here in Hampstead than they were in London, if memory served. It was not the stars but a noise that had roused him: a scurrying far too loud and frantic to serve a mouse or even the largest rat. He swiped a hand across his eyes and glanced toward the tray of food with its pot of tea, now long cold. A pair of bright green eyes blinked at him. The white feline behind those eyes went back to polishing off the remains of Theo's…luncheon?

"If the lady of the house discovers your presence, Linnaeus," Theo warned as he snatched a last piece of cheese from the edge of the plate, "we shall both be dining in the stables. Especially if she also learns you are allowing a rat the size of a small terrier to chase about the glass house."

The light-footed scamper, which had dragged him from his slumber, bore no resemblance to the heavy thud of the cat's languid pace. Linnaeus never hurried, not even in the pursuit of food. And he held himself in too high esteem to ever consider vermin or anything less than a dish of cold chicken as food fit for his discerning palate. Of all the possessions Sir Stirling's inestimable footman had managed to rescue from the Countess of Mulhaven's wrath, Linnaeus had been the most surprising and, as much as Theo hated to confess it, the most welcome.

As he straightened and pressed his hands to his back, a heavy quilt slid from his shoulders to the floor. Someone had come into the conservatory after he fell asleep and covered him against the barely noticeable cold. Was one of the maids sweet on him? Heaven help him, as that was the last thing he needed. Perhaps it was Mrs. Styles. Firmly in her mistress's corner, she still managed to toss conspiratorial winks and brash encouragement his way.

It was of no matter. Theo had come to look upon any kindness with suspicion over the last several years. Kindness always came at a price. One he did not care to pay.

"I'll not sacrifice the meager tatters of dignity left to me to wrest a bit of food from you, sir," he said to the cat, pushing a few slivers of ham under Linnaeus's batting paws. "I'm off to the kitchens. I suggest you find a place to pass the night." A scrambling across the stone floor had him peering into the darkness at the other end of the glass house. Linnaeus did not lift his head. "Your days here are numbered if the new Lady Grindon discovers how useless you are concerning large vermin assaulting her father's plants."

Theo toed off his boots, lit a single candle, and padded through the darkened house in search of something to eat before he found his own bed. Fortunately, his banishment to the ground floor meant his odd mealtimes were easily served. A quick traversal of the entrance hall and the east corridor put him at the baize doors into the main kitchen where he was certain to find—

"Sir Theo." A familiar, prim voice stopped him in his tracks. "Is there a reason you are creeping about the house at midnight in your stockinged feet?"

He mustered a carefree grin and turned to face his wife. His mood shot from false indolence to burgeoning curiosity. In his experience, women were who they were. Even those who acted the part of the siren or the lady-in-distress or the demure young girl just out of the schoolroom never managed to hide their true colors. At least, not from him. Eden Turner, however, was a chimera of women—all true, all opposed, and all as ephemeral as storm clouds during an English spring.

She stood in the corridor, candlestick in hand, dressed in a light-colored night rail, from which the cuffs and hems of an equally light hued nightgown peeked. She had some well-worn mules on her lovely feet in deference to the nighttime chill, and her hair hung in a single, long braid over one shoulder. As ridiculous as it sounded, especially to Theo, she presented the image of an angel. For a few seconds—with a bemused half-smile caressing her lips and a glimmer of concern in her tone—he almost believed this might be who she truly was.

She brushed past him into the kitchens and said over her shoulder, "You do realize your late-night visits to Mrs. Deeds' domain are a rude inconvenience to her and any number of the other servants?"

Theo closed his eyes and dropped his head as he shuffled behind her. She was an angel, to be sure. Until she opened her mouth. "I am unaccustomed to keeping regular hours when I am working, Lady Grindon." He headed into the pantry only to have her bump into him on his way out.

"You do not keep any hours at all, sir. At least, none I can discern. Sit." She indicated a bench at the long wooden table in the middle of the kitchen. He sat and stretched his feet toward the main hearth where a healthy fire still burned. "Neither do you eat nor sleep every day. Servants need consistency in order to do their jobs well." She rattled around behind him, efficient even in the noise she made in the darkened room. By the time his eyes grew accustomed to the light provided by the fire and their two candles, she slid a bowl of cold stew and a thick slice of buttered bread before him. A stone tankard of ale followed. "Eat," she ordered. "I'll return in a moment."

"As you command," he muttered and began to devour the stew. Lamb, with potatoes and carrots. It was quite tasty cold. Hot would likely be beyond excellent.

How did she know whether he ate or slept? The servants might need consistency, but apparently, they still had time to gossip about the habits of their mistress's new husband.

Eden returned and dropped a pair of men's Persian slippers at his feet. "Put these on." They were new, fawn gold in color, and lined in thick sheepskin. "If you continue to sneak about barefoot, you'll catch your death." She took his empty bowl and disappeared from the candlelight only to return bearing a plate with a slice of pie and a wedge of the superior cheddar he'd eaten in the morning's sandwiches.

"That might prove convenient for a woman who was forced to acquire a husband and now finds him such a trial," Theo said before tucking into the apple pie.

"Not as convenient as one might think."

He paused, a forkful of Mrs. Deeds' culinary delight halfway to his mouth. Eden stood at one of the sinks, her back to him, busy washing the empty bowl. An eerie finger of some raw emotion poked beneath his ribs. He finished the pie and cheese in silence, washing it down with the last of the ale. Once he slid his feet into the slippers, he gathered his dishes, rose, and brought them to the sink.

"Thank you," he said as he took the cloth from Eden's hands and began to wash the empty mug. "For the food and the slippers."

"Creevy sent Charlie to Town after the slippers," she replied.

"Your butler took it upon himself to provide me with fleece-lined slippers." Theo did nothing to hide his disbelief as he dried the dishes and returned them to their proper places.

She gave a little huff, which he found far more endearing than he should. "The price of a pair of slippers is far less than hiring another downstairs maid in order to keep up with your proclivity to drag half a field of soil through the house." Eden hurried around him and made for the door into the corridor.

"So much for concerns about my health." Theo sat back down on the bench and waited for her to turn around and look at him. He tugged the leather-bound journal from his waistband and dropped it onto the table. "What of your health, Lady Grindon? As your husband, I bear a certain responsibility for your health and safety, do I not?"

"It is none of your concern," she snapped, as she faced him. "But I always enjoy excellent…health." She stared at the journal and licked her lips. "Where did you find that?"

"The same place I found this." He drew an unmarked but expensive envelope from between the pages of the journal and tossed it across the scarred wooden surface between them. "Sir Stirling acquainted me with the manner of your father's death."

Eyes wide and startled, she lunged for the missive, but his hand was quicker. He turned the envelope over but did not open it. "This isn't the only one, Eden. The stationary bears no crest, but it is costly, and the hand is precise and well educated. The dates of the ones I have collected precede Dr. Turner's death. These are the reason he—"

She mashed her fingers to his lips. "It is of no matter. And I have no wish for the servants to overhear this discussion. They loved my father, but their loyalty to me is tenuous, at best."

Theo sat utterly still, savoring the press of her fingertips. He saw the moment she sensed his reaction. He fought a smile when she squeaked and snatched her hand away.

"You did not answer my question," she said, then sat on the bench across the table from him.

"Your question?"

"Where did you find my father's journals?"

"In a chiffonier in my laboratory."

"*Your* laboratory?"

He raised a brow. "The notes are the reason for your father's death. Which is the reason you had need of a husband with nothing to lose."

"There is always something to lose, sir. Sometimes we are simply late in seeing it. The reasons for our marriage are no one's concern save our own. The fact we are married means the Crown cannot seize my father's estate. My home and my income are safe, and for that, I am grateful."

"Our marriage also means the Duke of Arden cannot sue your father's estate for the death of his son and heir."

Her expression never faltered, but her eyes and the tightness around her mouth answered his question. And offered several more. Something sharp and strange turned over in his chest.

"It would appear you read quite a few of the notes you found."

"I read them all and most of the journals, as well. Your father was a brilliant man. In spite of the gossip, I do not believe he was responsible for Arden's heir's death."

"My father was too clever for his own good. And perhaps you would care to convince His Grace of Arden of my father's innocence. I wish you luck." She made to rise from the bench. Theo covered her hand with his.

"Have the notes stopped? Is the duke addressing his threats to you now? I am not without resources. Arden is a powerful man, but he is no match for Old Nosy himself."

She would be the sort of woman to smile at the mention of the Iron Duke. "You are acquainted with Wellington?"

"Served under him for eight years. He knows me well enough. I might avail myself of his influence, if needed." Theo had done everything in his power to put his military service behind him. He'd call upon it if he must.

"Then you are not merely *Sir* Theophrastus, you are..." Her voice rose with inquiry.

"I *was* Captain Grindon. I have no use for a rank I never sought, doing a job I never wanted, for reasons that proved an utter waste in the end."

"And those reasons?"

"Do not bear discussion. Some things simply don't."

She nodded and drew her hand from beneath his. "Agreed. Shall we add the notes you found to the list of things that do not bear discussion?" She stood and glanced about the kitchens as if his answer did not matter.

He was not fooled.

"If you wish." He pushed to his feet.

"I do." She went to the kitchen door and pushed it open. "I also wish you would take your meals on a regular schedule and confine your sleep to your bedchamber, also on a regular schedule. When you neglect your meals and fall asleep at your desk, or at your worktable, it makes extra work for the servants and disrupts their daily tasks."

He followed her as she lit their way into the entrance hall. "I shall endeavor to be a better tenant, my lady, for the sake of the servants."

"Thank you." Eden went to the young footman nodding off in the chair by the door. She nudged him awake and murmured something which had him shaking his head until her tone grew sterner. The lad shot out of his chair and scurried to the door behind the staircase which led to the steps to the servants' quarters. When she returned to Theo, he took up her hand and kissed it.

"And for the sake of the lady of the house who wanders about covering sleeping botanists, feeding said botanists when they go in search of a midnight repast, and sending same off to bed with a new pair of slippers."

She gazed up at him, her eyes more silver than grey in the candlelight. Confusion flitted in those silver depths. Her thumb brushed absently over his knuckles.

"Promise me, Eden, should you receive further notes from Arden, you will tell me. I have brought little to this marriage, but I would offer you my help should you need it. Promise me." She tried to tug her hand away, but he held fast.

"You are in no position to…" She gave the little huff he

found so ridiculously alluring. "Very well. Should I receive any further notes from the Duke of Arden, I will inform you at once, *husband*. Good night."

Theo watched her ascend the stairs. He curled his toes in the thick fleece of his new slippers. There was no doubt in his mind, Eden had been the one to drape the quilt over him whilst he slept. She'd sent the young footman to bed, and when Creevy chastised the young man for leaving his post, Theo did not doubt for a moment Lady Grindon would accept responsibility for the footman's actions. She worried about added work for the servants even as she attributed their devotion to duty to their love of her father, not of her.

His wife was a fraud.

Theo had his work. He was finally free to do it. Free to spend his days unraveling the mysteries of barley cultivation and the improvement of wheat cultivation. But the greater mystery had just climbed the main stairs of Longbow with a graceful sway of hips certain to haunt his dreams for the rest of the night. Worse, he suspected she was hiding far more than he'd even begun to imagine.

Dammit.

CHAPTER 5

For what I have lost, you will lose all.
There is no forgiveness for which you can beg.

Eden returned the note to its envelope and stuffed it into the drawer at the back of her desk. She locked the drawer and hurried to the mantel to hide the key. Any moment one of the servants would return to her chambers for the tray on the hearthside table. She poured herself another cup of coffee and subsided into the chintz chair to sort the post Creevy had delivered less than an hour past.

Not that there was a great deal of post to sort. Miss Eden Turner, daughter of the physician to the most noble families in England, had received countless invitations daily. Miss Eden Turner, daughter of the physician who had murdered a duke's heir with his incompetence, received none at all. Becoming Lady Grindon over a fortnight ago had done nothing to change that. She sipped her coffee, savoring the dark, biting taste, and contemplated the difference a few weeks might make in one's life. The difference an absent-minded botanist might make.

The one thing she had hoped would change had not. She'd received two notes since her marriage. Mixed in with an invitation from Sir Stirling's wife and a non-congratulatory missive from her father's only nephew concerning her marriage, they'd been easy enough to hide. As easy as all the others she'd received since Father's death. Did Creevy know? He was the one other person to touch the post. Did he wonder at the sealed letters with no identifying crest or frank? And now there was a supposed *master* in the house. Did Creevy inform *him* as to the contents of the silver salver the butler fetched above stairs from the ebony Chinese table in the entryway?

"Very well. Should I receive any further notes from the Duke of Arden I will inform you at once, husband. Good night."

She'd kept her promise, after a fashion. And she'd hardly slept a wink in the week or so since she'd made that promise. She had, however, managed to avoid her husband, save for the notes she took a secret pleasure in sending him throughout each day. His pithy responses made her smile, and she, pitiful creature, looked forward to them. So much so, she pressed the servants for complaints, inconveniences, and details about his days and nights closeted away in the conservatory. Simply to give her an excuse to send him a note.

In fact, this morning, Mrs. Deeds had complained to Charlie, the footman, of three untouched trays of food fetched back from the conservatory. Which meant Eden had a duty, once she'd finished her coffee, to pen yet another brief missive of chastisement to—

Slam!

Her bedchamber door burst open, and Eden choked on

her coffee, spewing it all over her slate blue morning dress. She shot to her feet, still coughing.

"He's found George."

"Mrs. Styles, for the love of God," Eden begged, once she recovered her voice. She snatched up a serviette and attempted to blot the hot black liquid from her bodice.

"Don't blaspheme. You have enough trouble on your plate." Mrs. Styles took the cup from Eden's hand and dragged her toward the corridor. "Sir Theo found George."

Eden tossed the serviette back into her library as she half-ran behind the housekeeper. "What do you mean he found George?"

They made short work of the corridor and stairs and soon arrived in the main library on the ground floor.

"I mean," Mrs. Styles continued, once she caught her breath, "he is in there demanding to know what the devil George is and why he is in the conservatory. And how is he ever going to fetch his cat down from the top of the banana trees."

"His *cat*? What cat?" Eden raced to the sliding doors and flung them open. And nearly slammed them closed. A scene of pandemonium only a ferment of men might create assaulted her vision.

"Pip, lad, stay away from that mangy beast," Her steward's command came from behind a wall of ferns.

"I am staying away. He's coming for me. I want down."

"Hold tight, Pip." This from Charlie, though Eden searched the immediate area for him to no avail.

Pip, on the other hand, clung to the topmost rung of a ladder in full display. The ladder seemed ready to dislodge him, the poor footman, or topple the swaying banana tree against which it propped. All this whilst the largest cat ever to cross her path yowled atop the thick fronds, putting the stormiest night on Hampstead Heath to shame.

Where the devil was Charlie?

"Hold fast, boys. I'll shepherd this creature away from the rest of us." Sir Theo, in bare feet, brandished a broom across the mosaic floor toward the camellias and belladonna plants.

Mr. Jobs trailed behind him shouting, "I wouldn't do that, sir. Lady Grindon will have both our heads should she— He's coming back this way. Watch for the—"

Crash! Only the destruction of one of the larger urns from Italy made such a musical sound when breaking.

The string of curses in the aftermath, however, could only come from a cavalry officer turned botanist.

Dear Lord, her younger servants did *not* need to learn new and more creative ways to cast aspersions onto the parentage of stray urns and disobedient felines. The language and the thrashing in the vicinity of the original crash did allow that her husband had not injured himself too badly.

One of the stable boys, Cal, if she remembered aright, bent over Charlie's arm with a length of cloth and a bottle of Mrs. Deeds' witch hazel potion. Eden marched to where Cal and Charlie stood. The long, deep scratches up and down the footman's forearm demanded her most immediate attention.

"Cal, allow me to take care of Charlie. You see if you can help Pip down before he falls and breaks something. Like his neck."

"Are you sure, my lady? That cat—"

"Is only a cat. Run along. I'll set Charlie to rights in a thrice and he can join you." She put paid to her words and daubed the pungent medicine onto the young footman's wounds.

"A cat the size of a bulldog with manners to match," Cal muttered, as he walked toward the banana trees.

"Jobs, for the love of King George and Napoleon's left ballock, do something with this beast." Sir Theo's voice came closer to Eden and the footman.

Charlie blushed bright red.

Eden patted his now bandaged arm and fixed him with her most somber regard. "See to Pip and do *not* repeat any of Sir Theo's gutter-born vocabulary."

The footman bowed, a puzzled furrow creasing his brow. "Vocaboo—"

"The words Mrs. Styles might clout your ear for using."

A broad grin of understanding bloomed across his boyish features. "Right you are, my lady." He loped off in the direction of the still shaky ladder and bent banana tree. Eden placed the bottle and bandages onto a diminutive wrought iron table next to a matching bench. Now to the heart of the matter.

Eden ran her hands over her skirts and rounded the wall of ferns to find her husband sprawled on his back on the floor next to an overgrown camellia. Leaves and bright pink flower petals covered his chest. In his fist, he clasped the long, curled, armored tail—

"George!" Eden cried. She stumbled, kicking the prone, ridiculous man in the ribs. With a few sharp slaps, she loosened his fingers and lifted George into her arms. It wasn't until she had checked her pet for injuries that she realized she was standing in such a way that her skirts covered Sir Theo's face and chest.

"I apologize, sir." She stepped back across him and snatched her skirts away in one frantic motion. "Jobs," she said, addressing her steward, "help Sir Theo to his feet. It cannot be good for him to lie on the floor, even if it is heated. And for goodness sake, one of you bring him his boots."

"No apology needed, my lady," Sir Theo said, one side of his mouth kicked up in a silly grin. He lurched to his full, considerable height. "Now, perhaps you can tell me *what* George is and *why* he has invaded my conservatory?"

Mr. Jobs, wise man, tugged his forelock and beat a hasty

retreat out the side doors into the ornate gardens behind the house. One of the young stable boys who'd come to watch the fun fetched Sir Theo's boots, dropped them at his feet, and followed Mr. Jobs to safety. Eden tried to step away from her husband whilst he redonned his boots. Unfortunately, he made quick work of it and ran to catch up to her. He cupped her elbow and steered her toward his work area. The one place in the conservatory she had no desire to go. She wrestled her arm free and strode toward the sliding doors and into the library.

"See to your cat, Sir Theo. Try to keep him out of the trees. I can little afford to risk the lives and limbs of my footmen to retrieve him every time he takes a notion to climb one."

"Pip will fetch him. He likes Pip. Linnaeus would not feel the need to climb trees," Sir Theo said, so close behind her, his breath tickled the back of her neck, "if his domain was not invaded by a giant armored…well, what the devil *is* he?"

She turned and glared at him. George struggled in her arms. Sir Theo folded his arms across his chest and met her glare with one of his own. Eden pursed her lips and glanced down at his muddy boots on the library carpets. He rolled his eyes, snatched off the boots he'd just put on, and dropped them on the rug.

"You did not tell me you had a cat." Eden settled onto the edge of one of the high-backed leather chairs before the fire.

"You did not tell me you had a whatever George is." Sir Theo dropped into the chair opposite her and waved a sinewy hand at her pet.

A sudden weariness swept over her. "He is a pangolin. The proper name is *Manis pentadactyla*. He's from China. Father gave him to me as a g-gift ten years ago." She wished to stamp her foot. Her throat and eyes burned. Why did he not go and find his cat and his boots and leave her be?

"George?" His tone of quiet amusement nearly undid her. His green eyes, somehow soft and strong all at once, steadied her.

"St. George." She ran her fingers over the grey scales of the creature balled up in her lap. How often she had envied his ability to shut out the world.

"Ah. The armor. I should have guessed." He reached over and touched one of the scales. George bristled, evoking a rattling noise. Sir Theo smiled with such charm, such benevolence…

"He won't eat," she blurted. "He has eaten little of nothing these two months and I d-don't know why."

"If it is any consolation, I believe he wished to eat me or perhaps Linnaeus before Pip and Charlie rescued us with a timely interruption." Sir Theo extended his hands and Eden placed her old friend in his cradled palms.

She drew a scant steadying breath. "He eats insects. Neither you nor the cat were in any danger."

Sir Theo's curious expression, somberly comical, eased the tightness in her chest. He carefully turned Eden's balled up pet this way and that, as if in search of an entrance. "I am pleased your mistress does not equate me with an insect, George." He addressed his statement to the long snout poking tentatively out of the rolled assemblage of wide grey scales. "I am not certain my tender feelings would survive if she did. Linnaeus, on the other hand, is immune to the opinions of others, good or bad."

"Fortunate feline," Eden murmured. Her eyes remained fixed on Sir Theo's hands as he used them to assess George's condition.

"Indeed. What sort of insects does George eat?"

"I'm not certain. There is some sort of large box of dirt in the east corner of the conservatory with a wide ring of water around it. George used to spend several hours a day digging in it, but now he seldom goes there, at all." Sir Theo held George out to her, and she settled her armored friend into her lap. "Jobs has the stable boys and the footmen scouring the countryside for insects, but George has shown no preference for them, at all. The insects, not the..." She dragged in a fiery breath to steady the pernicious quiver of her chin. "It is truly none of your concern. Your cat—"

"By now has either escaped the banana tree on his own or has eaten at least one of your footmen alive. Pity George has no taste for young men or day-old kippers." He leaned forward, his hands clasped between his knees and gazed into her eyes, his face more serious than she'd ever seen it. When she did see him, that is. "How long, Eden?"

"How long?"

He shifted forward and closed the space between them, so close the amber specks in his green eyes seemed to wink like tiny stars.

"How long have you had to care for everyone and everything at Longbow alone?"

"What nonsense." She shifted on her chair, which caused her skirts to brush his knees. His eyes widened and his gaze dropped to her mouth. Clutching a hissing, rattling George in her arms, she said softly, "George is my concern. He depends on me. We have been together a long time and..."

He raised a callused forefinger to catch the tear that rolled onto her bottom lip.

She drew in a deep breath as his palm curved around her cheek. "My father—"

"That's it." Sir Theo snapped his fingers and leapt to his feet. "Your father. Wait here." He took two long strides toward the conservatory, stopped, spun on his heel, and stormed back to her.

Eden stifled a gasp and half rose to meet him, George still cradled in her hands. Sir Theo clasped her shoulders, snatched her body flush against his, and kissed her. He tasted of tea and brandy. His lips, soft as velvet and as fiery and stunning as cannon fire, devoured and soothed all at once. Poor George hissed and struggled. Eden shifted him to one hand and ran her other hand up Sir Theo's arm and around his neck to slide her fingers into his hair. Incapable of breath or thought, she kissed him in return. To which he responded with a large step back, breaking off the kiss.

He shook his head and stared at her a moment. "What was I—" He snapped his fingers once more. "Wait right here."

"What was *that*?" Eden demanded.

He blinked. "A kiss?"

She rolled her eyes and settled George in the crook of her arm. "I know that. But why did you kiss me?"

He shrugged. "You were about to cry."

"I never cry."

He grinned. "Then I shall have to come up with another reason to kiss you. Stay. Here." He strode out of the conservatory, his grin lingering like a ghost at sunrise.

Eden dropped back into the chair and settled an unhappy George in her lap.

"Stay. Here."

Once her head stopped spinning, Eden had every intention of beating a dignified retreat to any room in the house save the one she now occupied. She rubbed her eyes and resisted the urge to touch her mouth, still hot and tingling with odd little shocks. He'd kissed her…fervently. That wasn't the correct word, but the correct word did not bear consideration. Nor did the order he'd issued as if she were a disobedient pup or a murder-minded cat. She gathered George under her arm once more and shot up on jelly-like legs. With determined steps, she made her way across the library toward the doors into the rest of the house.

"Stay here, my—"

The French windows into the conservatory clattered open. "I found it. I knew I'd seen the address in one..." Sir Theo glanced up from the book in his hand. "Where are you going?"

"I..." Eden took in his appearance. To the eyes of every Society matron, he was practically naked—no neckcloth, no coat, no stockings or shoes. His hair was a mesmerizing tousle of black silk. His eyes burned with an intensity that sent a delicious shiver down her spine. Oh, dear Lord, she had to get away from him at once. "I am going—"

He waved his hand, which sent ripples down the muscles of his arm, visible through the thin cotton of his shirt. "No matter. Fetch your coat."

"My coat?" *What the devil?*

"I had one of the footmen send for the carriage. Once he climbed down from the banana tree, that is." He glanced down. "I need my boots."

"Your boots? Why do we need the carriage?" She was talking to six people at once, all of them bedlamites.

"We cannot walk to London. Why have you not fetched your coat?" Sir Theo retrieved his boots and stockings from the rug before the French windows and sat down on a low table next to a blue and gold damask upholstered chair to don them.

London? Her skin went suddenly cold.

"London. I don't want to go to London." She stormed determinedly toward him. "Why must we go to London?"

He was on his feet so abruptly she had to stumble back. He walked around her to retrieve his waistcoat and morning coat from the large, square, leather ottoman where he'd apparently dropped them at some point.

"Because Nankin Street is in London. As the book says." He snapped his fingers and went back to where he'd pulled on his boots.

"Nankin Street? The book?" Eden sat down in the chair before the hearth. She'd grown dizzy trying to keep up with this conversation. If it *was* a conversation.

He bent over and rummaged beneath the table.

Dear Lord. His breeches fit like a second skin. Her father had been a physician. She'd studied the male form, but never had she studied a form like that of her husband. Greek and Roman statues had muscles there, *not* Scots botanists.

"Aha!" He straightened and turned; the book clutched in a hand over his head. "Nankin Street is where your father visited one Mister…Huang. Purveyor of Chinese herbs, Chinese medicines, Chinese plants. It's all in your father's journal. Most likely why he made this Mister Huang's acquaintance. The medicines. Sounds like a wonderful shop. It's where he found George, or, at least, that is what he wrote."

An eerie sense of dread crept into her mind, an insidious little vine of trepidation. "You read my father's journals? All of them?"

"Not all of them. Not yet. Interesting study. Come along. Bring George." He cupped her elbow, pulled her to her feet, and trundled her out of the library into the entrance hall. "Mrs. Styles!" he bellowed.

Eden, juggling George with one hand, almost dropped the poor creature. Suddenly, she wanted to laugh.

Creevy, a coat draped over his arm, stopped in his tracks, his eyebrows attempting to climb into his hairline.

Eden wrenched her elbow free. "Where are we taking George? Why are we taking George?"

The housekeeper trotted into the entrance hall, her cap askew and her eyes ablaze.

"To the shop in London. Limehouse, actually. On Nankin Street. There you are, Mrs. Styles. Can you send someone to fetch Miss Turner's coat and bonnet? We are mounting an expedition to London to discover what ails our friend George. Good man, Creevy. Thank you." Sir Theo took his caped great coat from Longbow's butler who offered the botanist a pair of worn leather gloves, as well.

"You, girl," Mrs. Styles barked at the downstairs maid who peered around the front staircase, no doubt drawn by the commotion that was Eden's husband. "Fetch *Lady Grindon's* black wool cloak, the one with the hood. Now, girl. Make haste." The poor girl scurried up the stairs like a jumped-up rabbit. Mrs. Styles, arms crossed over her hefty bosom, glared at Sir Theo. "*Lady. Grindon.*"

He stopped flipping through the pages of the journal and looked up. "Beg pardon?"

"She is Lady Grindon, now. Your wife?"

He furrowed his brow, which gave him such an appearance of boyish bewilderment Eden had to lower her head to hide her smile. Few could withstand Mrs. Styles in high dudgeon.

"Of course," Sir Theo finally said. He cleared his throat. "Quite." He turned his gaze on her, and his eyes widened. He tilted his head. Warmth spread up the back of her neck at being discovered as if in a child's game of hide and seek. When the maid returned with her cloak, Sir Theo handed the journal to Creevy and took the warm, woolen article to drape around Eden's shoulders. He closed the frogged fastener at her throat and drew the hood over her tightly pinned hair. He indicated the front door, held open by Creevy, and retrieved the journal as he escorted her to the carriage which awaited them under the portico.

Despite her utter dread, she allowed him to hand her into her father's entirely too ostentatious carriage. She settled onto the pillow-soft, dark blue velvet squabs of the forward-facing bench. To her consternation, a large lidded, wicker basket sat on the floor between the seats. She lifted it onto the seat beside her, opened it, and placed George on the bed of clean straw therein. The carriage creaked and leaned toward the house as Sir Theo hoisted himself in and dropped onto the seat behind the horses. Eden rested her hand on the basket as the coachman whistled the team into motion. She glanced at the basket and raised an eyebrow.

"Charlie thought George would be more comfortable," Sir Theo said dismissively. A slight flush crept up his throat.

"Charlie did."

He shrugged. "I've forced Linnaeus to travel a great deal. He prefers a basket." Her husband shifted on the seat as the carriage turned from the drive onto the road toward London. He propped one foot on his knee and stretched his arms across the back of the seat.

"Linnaeus is your cat? The cat whose existence you failed to announce to me before moving him into George's domain?"

"You had told me the conservatory was to be *my* domain once I put my head in the parson's noose. I had no idea I was to be a mere pretender to the throne."

Eden snorted. "I assure you, George would have proved a most benevolent ruler had a great hulking, clawed beast not invaded his kingdom."

"Dare I hope you are referring to Linnaeus and not..." That shadow of a smile flickered across his face.

Her stomach dipped. A fissure of irritation wiggled down her spine. She tightened her grip on the leather strap handles of the basket. "Why didn't you tell me about your cat? I would not have objected to his presence."

Sir Theo stared out the window. "I wasn't certain my..." He turned back to face Eden. "She was fond of him, or so I believed. I thought she might keep him."

"Ah." Eden was torn between sympathy for the man who believed he'd lost his pet and exasperation with the man who'd placed himself in such an untenable situation. "But she gave him his congé, as well."

"I suppose he reminded her of me."

"He's a tom cat, of course he did."

"Oh for… The lady threw me out because I made no time to bed her." He shrugged, though his face evinced more irritation than indifference. His eyes, however, evinced some odd emotion, something infinitely alluring in a manner both frightening and sad. She, never at a loss for words, hadn't the slightest hint as to a response and she could not, for the life of her, decide if she liked her speechless state or not. She tightened her lips and peeked in on George.

The whirr and crunch of the carriage wheels and the jangling of the harnesses were the only breaks in the silence. Eventually, the noisome tattoo of other carriages, wagons, and carts mixed with the steady beat of horses' hooves stretched Eden's nerves like the strings of a pianoforte tuned by too forceful a hand. She tapped a finger along the handles of George's basket. She'd travelled this road to London more times than she cared to remember— with her father to their house in Town, or to visit one of his wealthy patients, or to attend some social event to which she'd been invited for his sake. She'd gone to London once since his death, an experience she had no desire to repeat, yet here she was. All for the sake of a beloved pet and a whirlwind of a man she was bound to for the rest of her life.

"Eden?" His voice—dark and comforting as a quiet, fire-warmed room on a stormy night—jerked her from her reverie. She glanced down to find his hand resting over hers. His touch was light and tender in spite of the callouses and scars. She should pull away but had no power to do so.

"Are you well?" he inquired, rubbing his thumb across the back of her hand.

"I am not fond of London. You might have taken this errand up yourself."

"What if this Mister Huang has questions about George I cannot answer?"

"George is no great mystery, sir. He has not been tempted by food for a long while." Eden found herself the object of Sir Theo's intent study, as if she were some exotic plant. She swallowed as unobtrusively as she was able. "It is most disconcerting."

"It certainly is," he murmured, the brush of his thumb sending tiny rivulets of heat up the tendons of her hand. "A life without temptation is a very dull life, indeed. Don't you agree, Lady Grindon?" He sat back, and the skim of his fingertips across her wool-covered knee lingered long enough to evoke a shiver.

"I daresay you have experienced enough temptation for the both of us, Sir Theo."

"Not as much as you might think. Until recently." He shifted in his seat. A slight flush bloomed from beneath his ears down and across his throat. "What is your objection to London?"

"My last visit was after Father's death. I went to close up the house." To her consternation, she'd begun to grow accustomed to his sudden fits and starts, moving from one idea to another like a bee in search of the sweetest flowers. "One seldom learns one's place in society until a tragedy goes in search of a villain. If the first person cast as the villain is no longer available, any familial understudy will do."

"What happened?"

"My father was accused of murdering the Duke of Arden's eleven-year-old son. His *only* son. What do you think happened?" She faced the window—anything to avoid his gaze, which was interested and devoid of pity. Fortunately, in spite of the growing presence of buildings, people, and vehicles, she did not recognize this part of London. Anonymity meant a great deal to her in all things. From the smell, they were not far from the docks.

"It is my understanding your father was accused of incompetence, but no charges were brought against him." The even rumble of his voice… She turned her head enough to see him. His voice offered comfort when she wanted none. Needed none. Could bear none. And his face, handsome and earnest and growing each day more… Eden curved her palms around the leather straps of George's basket, tighter and tighter and tighter still.

"Is that what Sir Stirling told you? Try telling that to the neighbors and servants and gossip rag repor—" Her throat squeezed together. Her nose burned. Beneath her skirts, she kicked herself. "Reporters saiting at my doorstep to catch a glimpse of the murderer's daughter the last time I came to London." The carriage jolted and then rocked to a halt. Why are we stopping?" She half rose, released her grip on the basket, and reached to draw the curtain across the window. Eden had lied to herself. She didn't care where they were in London, she'd never be afforded the gift of anonymity. "Where are we? What—"

Sir Theo grabbed her elbows and gently lowered her back onto her seat. "I will tell you what Sir Stirling told me, Eden Turner Grindon."

"Let me go." She tried to wrest her arms free. His hands were gentle but insistent.

"After a long career as physician to the highest in the land, your father was thrown to the wolves for one mistake. And when he could no longer listen to their howls, he hanged himself over the table where I do my work. You found him there and had the forethought to cut him down and hide the manner of his death. More forethought than he had to leave you alone to deal with the loss of everything you own should his suicide be discovered. More forethought than he had to wonder if some distant cousin might present himself as your father's heir and make trouble for you. And more forethought than to leave you to deal with the wrath of the Duke of Arden and his army of solicitors."

"Father didn't know." Her throat tightened. "He didn't—"

"He didn't want to know. I do. Even the poorest excuse for a knight wishes to know what sort of dragons his queen might call upon him to slay, should the occasion call for it." His voice neither wavered nor rose a single note. He released her and reached to open the carriage door.

"I don't need a knight," she snapped. "I married you to protect my fortune. That is all. And the only dragon in my life is Mrs. Styles."

"The cousin, the law, and the duke I shall gladly face. Mrs. Styles, however"—he leapt to the cobblestones before the tiger had the chance to lower the steps—"you shall have to face alone."

"Coward."

He grinned at her.

A tendril of light seemed to creep into her shadowed life.

"Against Mrs. Styles? I daresay Lancelot himself would cry craven. Shall we see to St. George?"

Eden stared at the hand he offered to help her from the carriage. Her blood slowed and turned to water in her veins. She picked up George's basket and fought not to drop it as she handed it to…her husband, whose green eyes held a thousand things she did not want to know or see or feel. Sir Theo delivered her pet into the hands of the tiger and offered Eden his hand once more. He expected her to leave the carriage on legs like jelly with feet as immovable as the

Thames at the height of the Frost Fair. She picked up her skirts and placed her gloved palm in his.

"Why are you doing this?" she asked.

She hadn't the faintest idea to which *this* she referred.

CHAPTER 6

To Theo's immense relief, the distinct ring of the shop's bell and equally distinct young man in front of the establishment's red and black door saved him from answering his wife. The man dressed in a collarless jacket and a pair of trousers of deepest black ushered them into the shop. He took Theo's greatcoat and Eden's cape to hang on an ornate coat rack carved in the shape of a fantastical tree. A small fireplace in the front corner of the shop served to dry coats and keep them warm for patrons. Eden murmured her thanks even as she glanced over her shoulder at Theo as if she awaited an answer to her question. Theo waited as well, but nothing came to mind. Nothing on which he wished to think overlong.

The interior of the shop was warm but not overly so. A long glass case formed an open square in the center of the shop. A wrought iron, spiral staircase in the corner of the shop led to a mezzanine floor ringed by a beautifully designed balustrade of ebony. A floor-to-ceiling bank of apothecary drawers lined one wall. The other walls, replete with rich amber wood polished to a high sheen, curved into a domed ceiling. Colorful Turkey carpets covered almost every inch of space not taken up by smaller glass cases scattered with artful randomness throughout the shop.

An older gentleman stood behind a counter in the far back corner of the shop. He worked a mortar and pestle, oblivious to the presence of customers, or so it seemed.

A mixture of dark and light scents filled the air but did not overwhelm the senses. Or perhaps it was the siren call of the *Convallaria majalis* Eden wore that pushed all other scents aside. He'd thought lily of the valley a delicate but rather innocuous plant until he'd spent many waking and most of his sleeping hours in a calf-eyed stupor at even the hint of it nearby.

A sharp dig into his side, like the sort a sharp, feminine elbow might make, alerted him to the fact he'd missed something. He winced. His wife and the young man in simple black attire gazed at him expectantly.

"Beg pardon?" seemed a logical response. Until the newly minted Lady Grindon huffed and rolled her eyes.

"How may we serve you today?" the young man asked for the second or perhaps third time.

"We'd like to speak with Mister Huang about our friend here." Theo took the basket from Eden, placed it on the glass case in the middle of the room, and lifted the lid. George rattled his scales but poked his narrow snout out to perform an olfactory assessment of his whereabouts.

"*Chuānshānjiǎ*," the young man murmured, his heretofore stoic expression softened by a gentle smile. Theo hardly blamed him. Eden's pet was most charming—when he wasn't chasing cats or wide-eyed footmen. "I am Tan Hunqua." He inclined his head. "I will find Madame Huang." He was on the far side of the shop and halfway up the staircase before Theo realized what he'd said.

"*Madame* Huang? Did you—"

Eden, George cradled along one arm against her ribs, wandered to the apothecary drawers. She perused the labels and even opened one or two with her free hand. Her skirts brushed the floor and gave her the appearance of some fey creature floating across the large Turkey carpets. Her dainty fingers traced a path across the labels. Theo fought the erotic shudder that chased down his spine. He folded his hands into loose fists only to shake them free in sudden consternation.

The touch of one drawer stopped Eden in her tracks. She drew back as if scalded and strode across the shop to the glass case and counter in the far back corner. The older man behind the counter lifted his head and smiled at her. His gnarled hands never stopped working that mortar and pestle. Theo strode to the wall and scanned the drawers where she'd stopped. A florid hand had written labels on each drawer in both precise Chinese characters and Latin terms. It was the beautifully penned Latin that confirmed his suspicions.

"What trouble are you borrowing, my dear Lady Grindon?" he muttered.

Theo joined her at the counter, where the bespectacled man engaged her in a congenial conversation as he added dried herbs to those he'd already ground. Theo would never have guessed the man's age had it not been for the white hair hanging in a long braid down his back. He acknowledged Theo's presence with a slight sideways nod but did not divert his attention from Eden's earnest queries.

"Gin?" she asked, shifting George from one arm to the other. "I never thought to use gin. I have always used vinegar when making a tincture of belladonna."

"Ah. A good choice," the older man offered. "Gin is cleaner and makes a more efficient tincture." His features identified him as Chinese, but his speech held only the barest hint of anything other than the King's English.

"I shall remember that," Eden replied. "Thank you."

"I daresay her footman, Charlie, will be grateful, as well. No young man wants to go about smelling of vinegar. Gin, on the other hand..."

The apothecary, for that had to be the man's profession, chuckled.

"How did you know?" Eden asked, her inquiry laced with both shock and chagrin. The blush to her cheeks soothed the sharp edges of her normal expression. She appeared innocent and worldly all at once.

"He had an earache and then he didn't. He said you gave him some medicine to put in his ear and made him memorize the instructions."

"Very wise," the apothecary murmured.

"Belladonna can be dangerous," Eden said, her chin raised at the defiant angle he'd come to recognize as part of her armor against the world.

"Many medicines can be in the wrong hands." He wanted to kick himself the moment the words left his mouth. *Damn. Damn. Damn.* "Eden, I—"

"Miss Turner?"

Theo and Eden turned as one to find a Chinese woman, not young, but not yet old, with intense dark eyes of the sort that missed nothing. Two ebony sticks topped with exquisitely carved jade dragons held the silken mass of her black hair in an artful chignon.

An odd sense of familiarity tapped at the back of his mind. She was only a little shorter than Eden, but the energy she exuded put him in mind of another meeting.

Eden tossed him a pitying glance. "*Mister* Huang?"

"I—" Theo offered the shop's obvious proprietress a bow. "Dr. Turner's notes indicated..."

Good God, these two women, his wife and the quietly imperious proprietress, were frightening in their expectant silence.

Clarity slapped him like an irate mistress. Little wonder the Chinese lady's appearance evoked familiarity. Two sets of fierce, feminine eyes fixed him in place. He was a large, competent rat trapped between a pair of far more lethal, competent cats. Cats accustomed to ruling their kingdoms with a refined but iron hand. Two sides of a rare coin. He needed to tread lightly lest he become dinner.

"I do beg your pardon, ma'am. Sir Theo Grindon, at your service." He bowed once more, which the lady acknowledged with a regal inclination of her head. His wife regarded him with such gravity it nearly broke him, until he saw the crinkles of silent laughter at the corners of her eyes. "I simply assumed *M. Huang* meant *Mister Huang*. Foolish of me."

"Not at all, Sir Theo. We are all allowed a bit of foolishness now and then."

"Some of us abuse the privilege," Eden murmured as she shifted her pet in her arms.

"And may I make known to you, Lady Grindon"—Theo pressed a hand to the small of Eden's back—"my wife." He braced for an elbow to his ribs that never came.

"I wish you both very happy," Madame Huang replied. "It is good to have some joy in the midst of your sorrow. Your father was a true physician, Lady Grindon, and a good man. His death brought much sorrow to our community."

"Thank you." Even as she said it, Eden drew her shoulders back and raised her head. George stirred and sent a series of distinct rattles into the sudden silence. Theo brushed his thumb across his wife's spine, his reward a tiny give in her rigid posture.

Madame Huang held out her hands. Theo lifted the pangolin from Eden's grasp and delivered him gently into the other lady's cupped palms.

"Ten years," she observed. She moved to one of the long

glass cases and placed George on its polished teakwood counter. "You have done well with him. I know of no other Anglo who has kept a *Chuānshānjiǎ* alive and happy so long." She examined the creature with the same practiced intensity as Theo had seen in cavalry surgeons in battlefield hospitals.

"He isn't happy," Eden said. The tiny wobble in her voice caused Theo's heart to twist in a manner it never had before, which terrified him. "He won't eat. Father had a part of the conservatory set aside for him, but he has not gone near it these two months."

Madame Huang reached for one of Eden's hands, squeezed it, and called to Tan Hunqua, now busy with a stack of papers at an oversized desk near the shop's door. He hurried to the proprietress's side, listened for a moment as she spoke, and hurried back to his desk. Eden glanced up at Theo. He offered her a reassuring grin.

"Dr. Turner's collection of Chinese plants is quite impressive," Theo said. "Especially those with medicinal properties. His *Nelumbo nucifera* were obviously cultivated to make use of the roots. Am I correct in assuming he found most of his plants and a great many of his medicines here?"

Madame Huang smiled. "Your husband is a botanist, Lady Grindon. And a knowledgeable one, at that. And perhaps a physician, as well?"

"No." Eden walked a few steps away. The vehemence of that one word rebounded off the domed ceiling and startled both Theo and Madame Huang into an awkward silence.

"My paltry healing skills are reserved for sick plants," Theo finally said. "My lady wife is the dispenser of medicines at Longbow."

"Like her father," Madame Huang observed.

"Nothing like my father." Eden turned her attention to her pet, now rolled up on the glass case. George unfurled at her touch. "I make use of a few herbs and safe concoctions.

Things any well-schooled chatelaine might know. My father's hubris had him attempting cures with plants that were a mystery to other physicians. It led to his…ruin."

The tinkling of the bell over the shop door drew their attention to an exquisitely dressed lady who hurried to the counter where the white-haired apothecary still worked his mortar and pestle. He acknowledged the lady with a sharp bow of his head and then glanced at Madame Huang. Theo caught the nearly imperceptible motion of her hand to the employee. The lady leaned over the counter—her words low but her tone urgent, insistent. No matter her words, the apothecary demurred until the lady stormed out the way she came.

"Medicine sometimes needs to remain a mystery," Madame Huang said, her gaze still fixed on the door that had slammed shut behind the lady. She shook her head and turned to Eden. "Your father respected the medicines he used, but he was far too trusting. One might share the mysteries, but respect cannot be shared. It can only be learned and often at a terrible price."

Eden stilled. Theo did not detect even a flutter of breath lifting her chest. Something passed between her and the elegantly commanding shop proprietress.

"The lady who just left. Why was she refused?" Eden gathered George into her arms.

Theo resisted the urge to give his head a violent shake or three. He'd been dunked into a conversation with as little direction as a man pushed into a Scottish loch. What was this about?

"Her physician made the mistake of telling her the source of the treatments he administers. He shared the mystery."

"But not the respect," Eden finished for her. "Did the Duke of Arden…" Her voice faded the moment she glanced at Theo, as if she suddenly recalled his presence. He studied the women, each in turn. Unspoken words flew between them, unspoken questions. He went over the last few minutes in his mind. Confusion turned to suspicion and then to a sliver of an idea.

"Your refusal of the lady was a wise choice," Theo said with pointed precision. "An easy one. A duke, however, is another matter, even for a woman as wise as you, Madame Huang."

Beside him, Eden drew an audible breath.

"A wise woman knows which battles to fight, Sir Theo, and which to avoid," Madame Huang replied. "Fortunately, I never had an occasion to deny the *Duke* of Arden. It is said he knew little of his son's illness and cared to know even less."

"A damned fool," Theo muttered.

"A fool's sword can kill as easily as a scholar's. Remember that, Lady Grindon." Madame Huang raised her hand slightly to acknowledge Tan Hunqua, who had reentered the shop from the front door. She tucked her arm through Eden's and led her toward the entrance. Theo followed, his brain a stew of puzzle pieces with no clue as to where to begin to assemble them.

Young Tan held a carved, wooden box the size of a large kettle. He opened it as they drew near to reveal a glass bowl with a fitted glass lid. Inside were rich brown wood shavings, which appeared to be moving.

Theo reached for the lid only to have Madame Huang cover it with her palm.

"Not until you return to Longbow, I should think. Tan has arranged to have George's feeding box repopulated, and we will speak with Mr. Jobs to make regular deliveries. It seems this was something your father did personally, and once he was…gone, there was no one who knew to order George's food. A clerical error, for which I must—"

"Nonsense." Eden drew herself up and schooled her

features into the austere mask Theo had come to hate. "It was simply one more thing my father left undone. One of many."

"What precisely are they?" Theo waved at the box as Tan closed it. "What does George eat?" He put his hand on the pangolin's scales and his wife's attention followed. Eden might have donned her armor, but her words had hummed through him as clearly as the heat of a coming storm. He wanted to draw her away from the hurt of memory and doubt.

"*Báiyǐ.*" Tan handed Theo a sheaf of papers. "Wood ants."

"Wood ants? How will we keep them from eating the house?" Theo was not terribly sanguine about sharing his conservatory with an army of creatures bent on the consumption of every inch of wood in the vicinity.

"The water," Eden said, her voice laced with dawning enlightenment. "And the beds of garlic planted around it."

"Very good, Lady Grindon," Tan said with a grin. "Your father was a clever man."

"He told me. When I was a little girl, he told me. I remember now." She shook her head against the memory or perhaps against the idea she'd ever been close to the man who'd left her alone to face the censure of Society.

Theo found it difficult to breathe. The floor shifted beneath his feet. At least, it did in his mind. Thoughts of Eden's valiant fight against the demons assailing her buffeted him like a persistent fist to the gut.

"Shall we?" He pressed his hand to the small of his wife's back and indicated the door Tan now held open.

Eden grabbed George's basket though she remained lost in thought as he guided her outside to the lowered steps of the carriage before she bothered glancing up.

Whilst Tan helped his wife into the conveyance, Theo turned to Madame Huang who had followed them onto the pavement between the shop and the street. "Thank you, Madame. For everything."

"Of course," the enigmatic proprietress replied. "You will protect her, will you not, Sir Theo." It was not a question.

"As much as she will allow me. Does she need protection?"

"We all do, Sir Theo, from enemies both real and imagined." She and Theo turned as one to watch Eden and Tan deep in conversation. "She is keeping secrets from you."

"Tell me something I don't know, Madame." He took the lady's hand and bowed over it. "I don't suppose you'd care to enlighten me?"

"Not my secrets to tell." She tapped the leather journal tucked halfway into his coat pocket. "But yours to discover. I suspect you already know that."

"And I suspect I need to discover hers sooner rather than later." He moved to climb into the carriage but not before he gave the coachman a destination. Had he not done so, he might have missed a hurried exchange through the carriage window between his wife and the expressionless Madame Huang.

Once he was settled onto the seat behind the horses, he reached up to knock at the small wooden door behind his head, and the coachman whistled. The carriage rolled forward and moved onto the cobblestone street at a smart pace. Eden settled George back into his travel basket, beside which the carved box now sat.

Theo stretched his arms across the back of his seat and watched his wife as she fussed with George's basket and then the ornate wooden container. Once she had exhausted those two distractions, she turned her attention to her skirts, her pelisse, her bonnet. Still, he took in tiny changes in her expression and the myriad emotions reflected in her eyes. Did she know the allure of Eden Turner Grindon *sans* her customary armor of measured disdain? She'd learned some-thing at Madame Huang's, something about her father's role in the death of the duke's young heir. It had shaken her enough to lower her guard with him, but he wasn't certain he cared for the way he'd gained such insight. Actually, he wasn't certain of a great deal when it came to his wife. Only that he did not want to take advantage of her pain when it came to the memory of her father.

"Is something amiss?" Only when she waved her hand across his vision did he realize the intensity of his study.

He had the good grace to clear his throat and look away for a moment. But only for a moment. "With me? Not in the slightest. What did you and Madame Huang discuss so secretly?"

"Secretly? One can hardly discuss secrets on a public street, sir." She leaned over to peer out the carriage window.

"In my experience, you ladies can discuss secrets in the middle of a riot in full cry, let alone on a busy street. I will never understand Wellington's insistence on all spies being men. The wars might have ended years earlier."

"How do you know he didn't?" Her arch tone elicited a bark of laughter from him.

"Well played, Lady Grindon."

She continued to look out the window as they made their way to Narrow Street.

"This is not the way back to Longbow." She sat back in her seat and folded her arms across her breasts. "Where are we going?"

"The Grapes is at the end of the street. I understand they make an excellent beef pasty."

"You want to eat? In London?"

"People do. I think I missed breakfast. A pasty is just the thing to stick with us until dinner."

"You *think* you missed breakfast." She adopted the tone of

a stern governess. Which elicited some naughty thoughts on Theo's part. "Your dining habits, though prodigious, are the most ramshackle it has ever been my misfortune to observe. How do you not *know* if you have breakfasted?"

He shrugged. "My work demands my full attention. It tends to set the passage of time at naught. I am certain I had breakfast at some point, but it is nearly midday. A pasty and a mug of ale will do us both good."

"I am quite certain Mrs. Deeds has prepared a variety of foods in the hope you might forego your passion for botany long enough to take nuncheon. Her kitchen is in a constant ferment to keep pace with your other great passion."

"My other great passion?" He leaned forward and propped his arms along his thighs.

"The contents of my larder." Her lips tilted up at the corners even as she took a moment to glance out the window once more. "I really would prefer we return to Longbow." The carriage came to a stop.

Theo did not give her time to protest. He opened the carriage door and leapt to the pavement before The Grapes. "Shall we?" He offered his hand.

She folded her hands in her lap. "I will wait here." Her lips flattened into a militant line.

"Nonsense." Theo leaned into the carriage, placed his hands on either side of her waist, and lifted her out and down to the pavement. "I have it on the best authority no one of any consequence visits The Grapes at this hour of the day. I'm starving. Surely you must be, as well."

He crooked his elbow and dragged her arm through to rest her palm on his wrist. He

entered the tavern, only slightly dragging his wife along with him. He seated her at a table before the front windows and made a hasty retreat to the chair opposite her.

"Not all of us are slaves to the dictates of our stomach,

sir." His wife bit the last word off into silence as the tavern maid came to ask their pleasure.

Theo ordered half a dozen beef pasties and two small beers. His best *for-the-ladies* smile and half a crown hurried the maid's steps back to the kitchens to speed their order along. Eden removed her gloves and slapped them onto the table's scarred wooden surface. Unspoken words brewed in her eyes and expression. Helpless not to, Theo grinned. His fingers tapped a lively tattoo. She leaned across the table and flattened his hand with hers.

"And I do not care who visits this establishment, consequence or none, at any hour of the day." If not for the flags of color across her cheeks and the alluring growl in her voice, he might have believed her.

"Hmm." He shrugged. "I am pleased to hear it. Whose dictates are you slave to, Lady Grindon?" Theo turned his hand over and wrapped his fingers around hers.

Her eyes widened. "I… What a ridiculous question."

"Is it?" He rubbed his thumb against the heel of her hand. "You tease me for my passion for botany."

"And food." She smiled the merest bit.

"And food. What of you, Eden? Do you have passions for which I might tease you?"

She tilted her head, her face a portrait in contemplation.

He hesitated to guess.

"Treacle tarts and anonymity," she finally said.

"Beg pardon?"

She'd caught him staring at her. An activity at which he'd grown to excel in the last few weeks.

"My passions. Tease away, sir." She removed her bonnet and placed it over her gloves. The tavern maid returned with their mugs of beer and saved him from having to respond immediately. They sipped their beverages in silence for a bit. The noise of the tavern grew as more people wandered in in search of a midday meal and a pint or three.

"Treacle tarts and anonymity," Theo said as he leaned across the aged oak slab and used his thumb to brush a bit of foam from her top lip. "But not medicine? I've seen your father's journals, Eden. Or rather, his journals and your commentaries. Very informed and insightful commentaries. Not the notes of a common secretary. Why did you—"

"Why botany? Why not…cookery?"

He breathed slowly. Which gave him time to accept and to tuck away a bit of insight for further contemplation. And time to decide.

"My grandmother. After my grandfather died and my father inherited, she stayed rather than abandon her conservatory and her gardens. I escaped the clutches of every governess and tutor to spend time with her. My father was furious. Wished me to pursue more manly pursuits like my elder brother." He shrugged. "He gave up once I went off to school and took firsts in botany and a number of other areas that had nothing to do with the Church."

"You have a brother." She gazed at him, curious and interested and without the censure in which he took such perverse comfort.

"*Had* a brother. He managed to whore and drink and gamble away most of the estate within six months of our parents' deaths. He put a pistol in his mouth two weeks before Waterloo and the Crown took possession of—"

"Everything that was left." She covered his hand with hers, bare skin against bare skin, and his body hummed like a rung bell. "Your grandmother?"

"The same typhus outbreak that took my parents. I was with Wellington fighting the Corsican. By the time someone thought to write to me, we were in Belgium. I sold out after Waterloo and returned to no home, no family, and—"

"No conservatory in which to carry on your work."

"Until now." Something twisted in his chest, painful and sweet.

"Until now." She squeezed his hand.

Theo turned their joined hands and tightened his fingers around hers. He never spoke of his family. Never. The room spun, tilted on the realization of how long it had been, how long he'd held onto the loss and pain. And regrets.

"Eden, I—"

"It would appear your shame knows no bounds, Miss Turner," a dark, cultured voice announced above the din of the noonday custom. "To show your face in public, at all, let alone in London, proves you are no better than you should be."

Theo erupted from his chair, knocking it to the floor with a deafening clatter in the suddenly silent room. "And what should she be, mister..." His fists clenched so tightly he suspected his nails drew blood. A frozen sense of calm washed through him in waves.

"Lord," Eden said softly, her eyes bright with unshed tears. "Lord Anthony Lowestone."

The uncharacteristic tremor in her voice cut him as surely as any blade.

"She should be as far from England as a ship might take her," Lord Lowestone replied, his gaze never leaving Eden's face. "I do not know what this strumpet has told you, sir, but you are in the company of a murderess. She—"

Lord Lowestone did not finish his sentence. He did, however, shout a colorful expletive as he landed on the hard tavern floor. Theo's blood throbbed in his brain. His hand pulsed with beats of pain. Eden's voice worked its way through the strange haze in which he was immersed. She tugged at his arm as he reached toward the fallen lordling.

"Theo, stop. He's the Duke of Arden's nephew."

"With a pedigree like that he should be in possession of better manners than to offer a lady such insult." Air seared in and out of his lungs like hot ash.

"Her father murdered my cousin," Lowestone shouted, as he stumbled to his feet. "She is no lady. She is—"

This time, Lowestone's head snapped back, but he managed to remain upright. He swiped at his bleeding lip with the back of his hand.

"She is my *wife*, you scurrilous guttersnipe. Insult her again and I'll be serving you grass for breakfast at Battersea Fields."

"Wife?" The man's eyes grew impossibly wide in spite of the increasing swelling where Theo's first punch had landed.

"Come away, Theo," Eden ordered as she dragged him toward the tavern door. "Come away."

He had a vague notion of her sending a young lad to fetch their coach and driver. By the time Theo was able to see or think on anything other than Lord Lowestone, Eden had bundled him into the carriage, given their coachman his instructions, and sent the boy back into the tavern with money for the meal they had not eaten. The carriage jerked into motion and sent Theo sprawling across the rear-facing seat. Eden braced herself, one hand on George's basket and the other smashed atop her bonnet to try and keep it on her head. Theo attempted to steady himself with a hand pressed to the closed carriage window. Pain shot up his palm and radiated from his knuckles all the way to his collarbone. The duke's nephew had a deuced hard chin.

"Let me see," Eden commanded. The watery wobble in her tone softened the customary edge of her voice. She snatched up his injured hand, but not before she whipped the back of her free hand across her eyes. She examined the back of his hand, scraped and bleeding. She produced a handker-chief from one of those secret places ladies hid such items and began to blot at the blood. Her attempts were sporadic as she continued to swipe at her eyes with swift, impatient strokes. She sniffled. A stamp of her foot followed an inarticulate oath.

"Eden?" A thousand questions pressed against his lips, but he had not the slightest idea which might be the right one to ask.

"I cannot believe you hit him." She drew in a shaky breath but still did not meet his eyes.

It dawned on him. "Of course, I did. He's made you cry."

She did look at him now. "You cannot go about drawing the cork of every man who makes me cry."

"Why not?"

Her eyes widened, causing tears to roll down her cheeks. Theo raised his free hand and brushed at them with the pad of his thumb.

"Why not, Eden?"

"Idiot," she whispered, then had Theo sprawled across the squabs of the carriage bench beneath her, kissing him utterly and thoroughly senseless.

Merciful heavens, he was warm. He tasted of beer—and peppermint?

Eden ran her hands inside his coat and over the rough brocade of his waistcoat, then traced the landscape of his chest, hard as marble. A tiny thrill ran through her at the rising and falling of such rapid breaths. He growled, his lips soft and hot. Dear Lord, how hot and seeking and delicious.

A sizzling pang of comfort swept through her. She did not know why. She certainly had no idea what she was doing, only that she didn't want to stop. Apparently, Sir Theo had no inclination to stop, either. He fell back into the corner of the seat and pulled her atop his half-prone body. Goodness, he was muscled and firm...everywhere. Eden blushed from her toes to her hairline. Worse, he chuckled darkly, as if he sensed her thoughts. The resonance of his laughter careened about her body and lodged in the naughtiest places.

She trailed her lips along the line of his jaw and down the portion of his throat not covered by his neckcloth. He was having none of it. He hauled her back up to sear his mouth to hers, devouring and then soothing. He peppered kisses across her cheek to the spot below her ear, where he touched his tongue to her flesh. Eden shivered. He nuzzled his way beneath the collar of her dress and ran his teeth along the tender place where her shoulder met her neck. She fought the moan he drew from her as surely as an archer drew a bow. Her hands fisted in the black silk of his hair that curled well over the back collar of his coat.

Wicked, wicked heat suffused every place her body pressed his. Heat that burned through her clothes as if she wore nothing at all. His hand wandered down her spine and curled around her bottom to pull her more snuggly into the cradle of his thighs.

She gasped and blushed all over again. She slid her hands to his chest and pushed upright. He covered her hands with his and gazed into her eyes. His eyes blazed—sunlight through the deepest of forests.

"I mustn't," she declared, once a modicum of sense returned to her brain. "You… You're…" He was her husband. Of course, she could. She wanted to, badly.

The sounds of the city faded. They were on their way back to Hampstead. Home. Hers and…his. He cupped her cheek and brushed his thumb across her bottom lip.

"You mustn't what? Kiss me? Drive me mad with the touch and scent of your skin?" He punctuated each word with a kiss to her chin, her nose, the place where her pulse fluttered beneath her ear. "Have your wicked way with me?"

"None of that." She waved her hand only to have it land gently against the side of his face. Even his cheek was sharp and hard beneath its comforting warmth. Still, she had not the strength to remove herself from her position pressed so close to him.

One corner of his mouth kicked up in a wry grin. "Had I

known engaging in fisticuffs with a duke's heir would elicit such a response, I'd have done so far sooner."

"You shouldn't have hit him. I am accustomed to society's less than good opinion of me." The carriage's steady rocking, the warmth of his body—desire sizzled and snapped along every nerve in her body, but a far more dangerous sensation came over her. Her heart teetered on a precipice. It raced and pounded beneath her ribs.

"You won't have to be *accustomed* ever again. I won't allow it." He leaned up and kissed her, a world of unspoken passion delivered from his lips to hers. He pulled his mouth away just enough to speak. "I promise you, Eden, no one will—"

No!

Eden scrambled back onto her seat so abruptly, Theo nearly fell atop George's basket and the carved box in reaching for her. When he attempted to steady her, she pushed his hands away. He half smiled, which slightly covered the hurt and confusion that flitted across his face. Her nose burned with the effort required to breathe whilst trying not to weep. Slowly, as if she were a wounded animal, Theo offered his outstretched palm.

She was so concentrated on his face, on any hint of anger —or worse, disinterested disdain—she had to look down to understand he'd slipped his hand beneath hers and held it there. His fingers closed around hers, inch by inch.

"Do you want to talk about it?" His voice enveloped her, drew her though she did not move.

She shook her head. "There is nothing to discuss."

"Isn't there?"

"No." She sat back, and still he held her hand. "And you must pr-pr..." She wished she might swear. He needed to stop looking at her, but she would not give him the satisfaction of saying so.

"What do you want, Eden? I will give you anything in my power to give."

How many times had she heard those words? From her father. From an earl's second son before her father's fall from grace. Words. Lies. Nothing.

"There is nothing you have that I want, Sir Theo. Least of all, promises you cannot keep. You married me and saved my fortune. That is the bargain we struck. I need nothing else. Especially not the sort of attention that comes of you beating a duke's heir senseless."

"I didn't beat him senseless. Yet. And I am happy you want no promises from me."

"You are?" Well that was rather lowering. She'd kissed him first, but he'd kissed her in return like he intended to offer her—

"Indeed. Because when it comes to Lord Lowestone, I make you no promises, at all. Ever."

Dear Lord, the primitive thrill of pride and lust his words evoked in her blood both horrified and fascinated her. His green eyes shone with the determination to do violence on her behalf.

"I promise you, Eden..."

Foolish, silly girl.

"You can release my hand now, sir."

"Have dinner with me."

"Wh-what?" She tugged but failed to loosen his grip.

"Tonight. Have dinner with me."

"I'd rather not." Sharing a meal with the man who had punched Lord Lowestone was the last thing Eden needed. "Now, release my hand."

"I'd rather not," he replied.

~

"Do you want to talk about it?"

She had not. Talked about it. Or anything else, for that matter.

She'd sat in that carriage, her hand enveloped by his, and uttered not a single syllable all the way back to Longbow. She'd turned her head and stared out the window, all the while feeling his eyes on her—warm, compassionate, and with not the least bit of censure.

Only in the entrance hall, once their coats and George had been spirited away, had he pressed a kiss to her knuckles and asked again.

"Have dinner with me." Not a question, yet not quite a command. He'd held her gaze and smiled when she shook her head.

She had not seen him since, and the hour was well past ten.

"I am happy one of us is enjoying his dinner," Eden said as she forced away her maudlin musings and watched the pangolin dig through the contents of the glass jar she'd dumped into the box of dirt in the far corner of the conservatory.

Despite the heated pipes, the stone floor on which she sat was cool now that the sun had set. It was just as well. Each time her thoughts returned to her husband, which they did with annoying frequency, a flash of bone-deep heat sent sparks of desire to parts of her body far too dangerous to contemplate.

She had enough danger in her life. Tucked into the day's post, Eden had found another note.

I will have my revenge.
The debt you owe is unforgivable.

.   .   .

Her threatening correspondent had read too many of Mrs. Radcliffe's novels. However, between the note and the curious remarks of Madame Huang—*"I might respect the medicine too much to bow to a ducal household. Not every apothecary in London has such scruples. Your father may be more victim than villain."*—Eden had done something she'd vowed never to do again. While George happily devoured the new wood ant denizens of his dirt kingdom, she dragged another of her father's journals into her lap.

More victim than villain? Had Eden cast her father in the role of villain? Perhaps. But not for the reasons one might think. Not in her heart of hearts, when she lay awake in bed and contemplated her lot in life. Of course, her thoughts had been of a more immediate and far less philosophical nature as of late. There was nothing philosophical about the wicked turn her dreams had taken. Wicked dreams about green eyes, a lopsided grin, and hands—

"I shall try not to be insulted that you prefer George as a dinner companion," a rich, deep voice intoned from a few feet up the tiled path.

Eden started; her heart set off at a gallop. The leather-bound volume slipped from her lap. Standing in the glow of one of the lamps scattered about the conservatory, Sir Theo defined wicked temptation. His hair appeared damp from a bath. He wore a quilted, emerald velvet banyan. The neck opened into a deep V accented by gold embroidery. The fine needlework was nothing compared to the expanse of tanned muscle exhibited by the gaping garment. It fell to his ankles in heavy folds, but his feet were bare. For some reason, she had no ability to stop staring at those long, finely shaped feet as they strolled closer and closer. When he reached the place where she sat, he used one of those feet to move the stack of journals aside and lowered himself to the floor next to her.

Say something, you ninny.

"I had little appetite for food or conversation. I fear I would not have been a pleasant dinner companion." She tried to pull the hem of her wool merino gown over her own bare feet, on which his gaze was now fixed.

"I am perfectly capable of dining with a silent dinner companion." He gently tucked her feet beneath his robe. "I've learned never to underestimate a woman's ability to remain silent when it suits her purpose."

"Her purpose?"

"To make a man grovel and beg for her forgiveness." He smiled a bit ruefully, the artist-carved lines of his cheekbones and jawline illuminated by the light of a lamp behind them.

"Ah. And did you have occasion to do so often?"

"Constantly." He picked up one of the journals and began to page through it with feigned disinterest. "Have you found what you were looking for?" He nodded at the stack of journals.

"Have you had your dinner?" She fought the need to share her ridiculous quest to make sense of her father's life. And his death. Eden had not trusted anyone in years, long before…

"Actually, the proprietor of The Grapes sent our pasties along. I ate a few of those before I enjoyed Mrs. Deed's excellent roast beef and potatoes."

"Of course, you did."

"There are four left if you—"

"No, thank you." She realized her feet were pressed against his calves beneath his banyan. Her attempt to withdraw them was stayed by his hand clamped over the velvet fabric, his thumb rubbing her arches. "You are very warm, sir. Rather like a furnace." She resisted the urge to clap her hand over her mouth. What a ridiculous thing to say. Even if it was true.

"I always have been. I have no idea why."

Eden suspected she did. Not that she dared say it or even think it. "My feet have always been like ice."

He laughed, a deep resonant sound she felt to her now-warm toes. "My mother raised me never to naysay a lady."

She tried to withdraw the offending appendages once more.

"Don't." He tucked the end of his robe tightly around her from her calves to the bottoms of her heels. "I will do my best to keep you safe, Eden, if you will let me. And I expect you to do the same for me. That is the least a husband and wife might do for each other."

He was so close. The air around them was redolent with the scents of damp earth, hyacinths, orange blossoms, and a hundred other plants and flowers. The lamplight gave him the look of carved marble—all the lines and curves of a warrior's countenance.

"What possible danger might threaten you?" she asked softly.

"I don't know, but I suspect we shall find out." He touched her face with his free hand. "Running out of food, perhaps?"

Laughter bubbled up like a kettle set to boil. She laughed until she could not catch her breath. Her chest hurt. How long had it been? How long without the unfettered freedom and joy of merriment? One of the many gifts this man had brought into her life.

No, she scolded herself. *No gifts. No expectations. No promises.*

Eden drew a steadying breath. "You did say there were four pasties left. How many did the keeper of The Grapes send?"

"Eight."

"Good Lord. You ate four pasties *and* a plate of Mrs. Deed's roast beef?"

"Two plates, actually." He rubbed his stomach.

Eden tried to ignore the stretch of velvet across the ripples of that portion of his anatomy. "I should have left off that second plate."

"Thanks to you, George has enjoyed a good repast, as well. I cannot imagine—"

"What do you hope to find in these, Eden? What are you looking for?" Theo dragged several of the journals closer and fixed her with an unwavering gaze. "What did Madame Huang say to you?"

She opened her mouth. And closed it again. The lightness he'd brought her began to fade. The weight of all she knew and didn't know draped itself around her like a shroud. A cloak of secrets, suppositions, and overweening pride—her father's and her own.

Theo sighed. He brushed his knuckles along her cheek. "Eden," he murmured.

"The Duke of Arden did not love his son, but he did not want him to die," she blurted—and found she could not stop. "The boy was sick, and the duke wanted him strong and healthy. He hates his nephew, Lord Lowestone. Has no desire for him to inherit the dukedom. Poor man's mother was a governess."

"She did a poor job of raising him," Theo said darkly.

"How is your hand?"

"Far better than the duke's nephew's face."

Eden snorted and rolled her eyes. "My father did everything he could to help the duke's son. The duchess was frantic. She doted on him so. She would have done anything to save him. I...simply need to know how far my father might have gone to keep her happy. The duke was his most prestigious client. Madame Huang..." She shook her head. "She warned me not to cast my father as the villain. I am trying to discover how the boy died and how my father treated him."

"Madame Huang is not the only apothecary in London,

but she may be the only one with the courage to refuse a duke," Theo mused. "Or a duchess."

"Her Grace was the boy's mother. My father was his physician. It would not be the first time he took a chance with a treatment." She began to stack the journals, not wanting to talk about the situation anymore. Not with him rubbing her feet and listening so attentively. Not with the simmering sensations dancing between them. She knew from the look in his eyes he no longer wanted to *talk*, either. "This would simply be the first time one of his treatments did not work. It is late. Thank you for helping George." She tried to stand.

"Eden, don't." He cupped her elbows and forced her to meet his gaze.

"I'm quite tired," she said, far more softly than she intended.

"Do you think your father killed that boy?"

Damn him. Damn all the reasons she'd let him into her life. Her throat burned.

"Is that what you are trying to discover, Eden? What you are trying to prove? Do you really think he killed Arden's heir?"

"I don't know," she shouted as she tried to push him away. "I only know my father killed himself." Tears welled in her eyes and slid down her cheeks. "He killed himself and left me to deal with the wreckage. He *promised* all would be well. He always did. It never was. And now it never will be again."

"My poor girl," he murmured as he took her in his arms. "My Eden."

So simple. So wonderful. So easy to subside into his embrace and soak in the strength and comfort he offered. There was peace in his arms, despite, or perhaps because of, a determined brook of awareness running full tilt from his body through hers. Unfortunately, his words penetrated that peace and sparked an indignant fear.

Eden flattened her palm against his chest and pushed. Her hand landed on the bare flesh beneath his robe. She pushed once more and found the beat of his heart, thundering against her skin.

"I'm not…a girl." Eden tilted her head up to look into his face. "I'm a grown woman and I…I…" There were tiny bursts of gold in his eyes. Something about the way he looked at her gave those bursts the glitter of fireworks. All the while, the strong pulse against her palm called to her heart to march in time.

"Yes. I noticed." He fisted one hand behind her back and drew her closer. "I've noticed it more and more of late." With his other hand, he drew a forefinger along her temple, across her cheeks, and then along the line where her hair met her forehead. "I notice everything about you, Eden. And I suspect you have not allowed yourself to show a moment's weakness in a very long while. You cannot blame a man for shamelessly taking advantage when you do."

"Taking advantage?" she said, breathing the words across his lips, scant inches from hers.

"Shamelessly." He brushed his mouth along her jawline until he reached her ear. "Absolutely." He nipped at her earlobe.

Eden shuddered. Her head fell back, and he caught it in his palm, sliding his fingers through her hair and scattering pins. His lips pressed kisses down the side of her neck and back up her throat. He captured her lips in a soul-opening kiss. Eden wanted to fight the need he evoked even as every ounce of will she possessed flowed from her body like rain. Oh, who was she attempting to fool? Only herself. She ran her hands inside his banyan and reveled in the sensation of sun-fired stone his broad chest and shoulders evoked. A dark groan rumbled up his body. He lay back, drawing her with him, until they faced each other on their sides. He teased and tempted and marauded her resistance with nips, kisses, and touches of his tongue to the seam of her lips.

Her fingers swept over his collarbones, up the corded lines of his neck, and into the thick, cool silk of his hair. She clenched her fists as if she might hold him forever through those silken strands. Her lips parted. His tongue surged in, only to retreat, trace her lips, and then foray inside once more. He licked the roof of her mouth, the sides, then slid his tongue alongside hers in invitation. The tentative flicks with which she answered that invitation sent such a shiver through him she wanted to cry out. She did cry out, making him shake and groan with need of her.

Madness. This was sheer and utter madness, and she was powerless to stop. He rolled her gently beneath him. Propped on his elbows, he continued his campaign of kisses. Some sweet and gentle. Others so deep, Eden had the sensation of falling into a storm-tossed ocean of fire and need. There was no time, no place, beyond the demands of his lips and the press of his body—his powerful thighs to hers, his chest brushing the sensitive points of her breasts the strained against the fabric of her dress.

She wanted him. She'd never wanted anything more. The sensation was exhilarating and frightening and…impossible.

She gasped and turned her head. Theo froze, save for his heaving chest.

"I can't," she whispered. "I can't."

"Eden."

She turned back to him and placed her hand over his racing heart once more. She wanted to touch his warm and comforting body one more time. "This was not part of our bargain. I'm sorry." She swallowed hard against the burning in her throat.

"I don't understand."

He didn't. She saw it in his eyes, in the way those golden bursts disappeared, replaced by…oh, she didn't want to contemplate what. She could not.

"I cannot. This was not—"

"Part of our bargain. As you said." He rushed to his feet and offered his hand. Once she took it, he pulled her up as if she weighed nothing at all and she crashed into his chest. The first, last, and only place she wanted to be.

He stepped back and dropped her hand. For a moment, he appeared to want to speak. He scrubbed his face with his palms and gave his head a violent shake. "You have me at a disadvantage, my lady. You have since the day I met you." A small, sad smile creased his lips.

"I…" Words crawled up her throat and crowded into her mouth but refused to go any further. The exotic scents, the damp heat, even the glow of the lamps dimmed, and the world became a faded watercolor. Everything, the events of the day, the shimmer of desire between them, slipped back into the darkness.

Theo caressed her cheek, his large, roughened hands tender and gentle. "But you have yourself at a far greater disadvantage, and I don't know how to get 'round it. More's the pity, I don't know why I suddenly, desperately want to. Good night, Eden."

Like a wraith, he disappeared into the foliage of the conservatory. The click of the French windows and then the thud of the heavy library door echoed in the quiet before Eden drew another breath.

She stumbled to the stone wall around George's fiefdom and sat down hard. Cold tremors assailed her arms and shoulders. She had not known how warm her husband was until he'd bid her good night and left her to the manufactured warmth of the conservatory.

"What have I done, George?" She allowed the singular creature to snuffle her fingers and then watched as he waddled away in search of more wood ants. She'd wished for the pangolin to have an appetite like...

A hot, wet tear slid down her face. She swept it aside and got to her feet. The scattered journals beckoned from the stone floor. Eden uttered a vulgar curse and kicked them aside. She headed to the end of the conservatory, where an inset door hid a staircase leading to the first floor.

She was glad she'd sent her lady's maid to bed. Eden hadn't the strength to behave as if her entire world was not crumbling around her.

Once in her room, she made quick work of wrestling out of her dress and into her thick cotton nightgown. She flopped onto her bed, staring at the cherub figures on the painted canopy above her head. The banked fire in her hearth cast weak light over the figures. Weariness settled over her like a quilt added to her bedclothes. Her last thoughts were of hooded green eyes, warm skin, and arms that made her feel safe in an unsafe world.

The latest note had stoked the flames of fear already consuming her. Yet her husband's kisses had done far worse. They had made her dare to hope. Something she could not afford to do.

"MY LADY. MY LADY, PLEASE WAKE UP."

What the...

Someone was shaking Eden's shoulder. Violently.

Eden fought her way up from flashes of a rather breathtaking dream. It took a moment or two for her to roll over and push into a sitting position. The light of a candle bobbed about in the darkness at her bedside. She blinked in an effort to focus.

"Mrs. Styles?"

Longbow's formidable housekeeper did not look as imposing in her night rail and cap. But what was she doing in Eden's chambers at this ungodly hour? The clock on the mantel read a bit past two.

"You must come quick, my lady. It's Sir Theo." Mrs. Styles shoved wool mules on Eden's feet, then pulled her off the bed to shove her arms into her favorite flannel robe.

"Sir Theo?" Eden's spinning head stopped. All sleepiness evaporated like smoke. "What on earth could possibly—"

"He's dying, my lady. Sir Theo is dying."

CHAPTER 8

HE'D FALLEN ASLEEP IN THE CONSERVATORY AGAIN. THEO could think of no other reason for the sweat pouring from his every pore beneath his clothes. The air was so damp, he had trouble filling his lungs. Someone had stoked the fires beneath the glass house entirely too high. He'd speak to Mr. Jobs, but not tonight.

He turned his head and tried to sit up. A serious error in judgement. His head throbbed and his belly burned, as if he'd swallowed hot coals along with that last pasty.

"Here now, sir, none of that," a familiar voice said.

Theo tried to focus on the face attached to the voice, but even in the bright light of the lamp on his bedside table, the visage was murky, at best. Bedside table? He wasn't in the conservatory? A vicious pain stabbed his gut. He moaned and rolled onto his side.

"Her ladyship is on her way, sir. Lie still." The lad paused before softly continuing, "He looks bad, Charlie. Powerful bad."

"Stubble it, Pip. Go and see what's keeping them."

A cool breeze wafted over him, only to disappear with the

slam of a door. Frankly, Pip's assessment was right on the mark as far as Theo was concerned. He *felt* powerful bad.

Theo and his brother had once purloined a large bottle of their father's best port. They'd spent the better part of that evening consuming the liquor in ever increasing quantities in an attempt to impress each other. And spent the wee hours of the morning praying for death. That was the last time Theo remembered feeling so ill, and he'd since been shot, stabbed, and suffered some sort of Spanish influenza.

He opened one eye and waited for the room to stop spinning. A young man in a simple footman's uniform scurried to his bedside. Charlie. He filled a glass with water and offered it to Theo. His burning skin willed him to take it. His roiling stomach said otherwise.

"Theo!" His chamber door burst open, bringing soothing air and a stern sounding angel in white.

"Eden." His throat was so dry her name was all he could utter.

He dropped his legs over the side of his bed and lurched into a seated position. Pain dug a searing claw into his abdomen and forced him to double over with a strangled moan. Gentle feminine hands pushed him onto his back. One came to rest on his forehead as she sat on the edge of the mattress and tried to pull the covers over him. He pushed the quilt and counterpane away.

"Theo, what's wrong? Where does it hurt?" she asked softly. The scent of lemon and verbena settled around him. His vision cleared as he concentrated on her face. With her hair in one long sable braid hanging over her shoulder and resting on his chest, Eden looked so young and so very beautiful.

"It doesn't hurt at all." He mustered a weak grin.

She rolled her eyes and pressed on his belly. "Does that hurt?"

Theo gasped and half-sat up. "It does now." Another sharp pain hit him, and he fell back onto the pillows stacked at the head of his bed.

"Light the other lamp, Mrs. Styles," Eden ordered. "I'd forgotten this chamber has no windows. Charlie, open the door into the library. It is too stuffy in here by half."

"If I—had rooms—above stairs—I'd have windows," Theo managed to gasp. The excess light produced by the additional lamp caused him to wince.

"He's white as chalk," Mrs. Styles whispered loudly enough to be heard in the stables. "He looks near dead, my lady."

"Thank you, Mrs. Styles. I feel much better now." Theo groaned and rolled onto his side. He drew his knees up to his chest.

"When did this start? Theo," Eden insisted as she shook his shoulder, "when did you first feel ill?"

Eyes closed tight, he drew in her scent and the steady, calming sound of her voice.

"Should we send to London for the physician?" Mrs. Styles inquired from across the room. Her heavy, shuffled footsteps moved closer.

A *thunk* on his bedside table jarred Theo's throbbing head. The swish of water and the noise of a flannel being soaked and wrung out did not prepare him for the welcome relief of the wet cloth being dragged across his face, his neck, and his shoulders.

"None of them will come, Mrs. Styles." The pinched tone of Eden's voice pierced the thin veil of pain clinging to Theo's very skin. She was worried. And hurt.

"I don't need a physician. It is merely something I ate."

"Are you saying our Mrs. Deeds has poisoned you with her cooking?"

"Not even at gunpoint, Mrs. Styles. I'd rather starve than insult Longbow's queen of the kitchens."

"She hears word of this, and you will starve," Charlie assured him.

"I have little appetite at the moment." He shifted again but found no comfort, save the continuous ministrations of his lady wife and her water-soaked cloth. She'd managed to pull his arms free of his banyan and bare his chest. Her hands trembled, but she continued to bathe him. She rested her fingers over the beat of his pulse behind his ear and then checked the same flutter at his wrist. Their eyes met, and the first hint of real concern entered his thoughts. "Perhaps I should not have indulged in that second plate of roast beef."

"Theo." Eden swallowed hard and bent to press a quick kiss to his lips. A quizzical expression crossed her features.

"And I didn't have to punch a single peer."

"Hush." She pressed two fingers to his mouth and leaned in as if she might kiss him again. A room full of servants and himself near death was not precisely romantic. And now, when it came to his wife, Theo wanted romance. Once his belly stopped trying to put a period to his existence.

Eden sat up abruptly. "What else did you eat this evening?" She glanced about the room. "Charlie, fetch me that box, if you please."

She pointed at the flimsy container in which the pasties from The Grapes had been delivered. The footman tripped over his feet to do her bidding. Once she had the box, she picked up the pasties and smelled them, mashed some filling out, and tasted it. Theo understood the inclination. What he did not understand was Eden's odd examination of what was left of what had been eight pasties. Another cramp bent him double, and he barely suppressed an agonized groan. He didn't want her to worry. He was becoming a bit concerned himself.

Especially once she ripped one of the remaining pasties in two and began to sniff it as if it were a posy of flowers. Her eyes widened. She glanced at the container once more, dropped the destroyed pasty inside, and motioned for Charlie to take it.

"Go to the back of the gardens," she instructed. "Burn this and bury the ashes as deep in the ground as you can. Do you understand?"

The poor footman's expression matched Theo's thoughts—confusion mixed with horror. "Yes, my lady." Carrying the container as if it were a dead rat, he brushed past Creevy, whose arrival Theo had missed entirely. A belly full of fire tended to do that to a man.

"Creevy, my father's medicine chest is in the study."

"At once, my lady." The butler bowed and left.

Eden addressed Theo, "I need a scrap of parchment."

He forced himself to point at the desk he'd moved into the far corner of the room.

She hurried over and scribbled something on a small piece of paper then conferred with Mrs. Styles in hushed, insistent tones. The housekeeper raised a hand to protest, but stormed out to do her mistress's bidding. At last, Eden turned to him. She glanced around the room, her hands clutching the worn fabric of her robe. Once her eyes met and locked with his, she opened her fingers and returned to his bedside. Only when she'd settled onto the mattress and reached for the cloth soaking in the basin on his bedside table did he notice how she trembled.

"Eden?" he rasped.

She rolled him onto his back and wiped his face with the flannel. "When did you take that last bite of pasty?"

He stared at her, his vision not quite clear. Blinking did not help. "I don't understand."

"You took a single bite out of one of those last four

pasties, Theo. Think. How long has it been? When did you start to feel ill?"

He licked his lips. His body ached as if he'd been beaten, save for the places she bathed in tender, featherlight strokes. "I tried to…eat one of the pasties…after I left you in the conservatory. I didn't feel sick until an hour—" He broke off with a gasp. Pain lanced across his back and around his middle. He rolled toward her in an attempt to relieve it. Eden swept the damp cloth across his bare back, draping herself across him as she did so. When she leaned back up to wet the flannel again, she gazed into his face, her eyes bright with unshed tears.

"I'm so sorry, Theo. You've been poisoned. A tincture of tobacco was mixed into some, if not all of the pasties." She tried to smile. "Thank God you are such a great hulk of a man, and you did not finish all eight of them or you would be dead already."

"Tobacco? I don't take tobacco. Never have. Nasty stuff." His head began to spin and throb. *Pasties? Poison? How did she…*

"One of your finer qualities," she murmured.

"I have more than one?" His throat scratched with every word, but dying or not, he did not intend to waste an opportunity to speak to her alone. In his bedchamber.

I really am a reprobate.

"You have a few." Eden looked over her shoulder. "Where are Creevy and Mrs. Styles? We must purge this poison from your body immediately." She continued to bathe his chest and arms, an occupation to mask her obvious concern and fear.

Purge? Not romantic sounding, at all. Someone had poisoned him. With the pasties from The Grapes. Poisoned him. He grasped Eden's wrist.

"The poison. You are certain?"

She avoided his gaze. "It was mixed into the meat in the pasty, but I smelled it. Your symptoms indicate—"

"Who would want to poison me, Eden?" He shook his head in spite of the pain. Theo needed clarity that threatened to elude him. He had to think, dammit. Something was very wrong. "Eden," he rasped. "Who would want to poison *me*?"

"You mean other than your three former mistresses?"

"Four. They would never poison me." He shivered, a cold sweat breaking over him in waves. His vision began to narrow in black curls at the edges. "They'd…shoot me."

She set to soaking the flannel and wringing it out once more, still refusing to look at him.

"Eden." He gasped and clutched his side. Instantly she was there, tucking a pillow behind his back. "What if you had eaten the pasties? What would have happened?"

"Theo."

"How ill would you be?" He flattened his free palm against her back and held her in place. "How ill, Eden?"

"Very." At last she turned her grey eyes to his.

Clarity came to him in an instant. He lurched up. Once. Twice. He'd stumbled off the bed onto wobbly legs before Eden stopped him.

"Are you mad?" She shoved against his chest.

"I will kill him," Theo muttered, as he cast about for his trousers. His banyan began to slide past his hips. "Lowestone is a dead man." He took one staggering step forward.

"Get back into bed, you great looby." Eden planted her hands on his chest and pushed. Whilst doing so, she stepped on the trailing belt of his banyan. They both looked down and then immediately up. Theo's legs chose that moment to give way. He fell back across his bed with a startled and perfectly shaped Eden draped over his naked body.

It was comforting to know, even half dead, the important parts of his body were alert and in good working order. Not a surprise, as for the past several weeks, Theo had found himself more and more convinced his wife had the power to arouse a dead man.

"You-you-you…" she spluttered as she tried to rise. "You sleep naked?"

He attempted his most rakish grin. "I—"

A storm of nausea sent him curling over the side of the bed toward the chamber pot someone had placed strategically next to it. Which sent Eden sprawling onto the floor.

"My lady!" The floor creaked as Mrs. Styles lumbered in, followed by Mr. Creevy, if the masculine throat clearing was any indication. Theo was too occupied dry retching into the chamber pot and trying not to fall off the bed. Creevy retrieved Theo's banyan from the floor and levered him back into the bed.

"See to Lady Grindon," Theo ordered, between grinding teeth as the butler dragged the covers over him.

"I'm fine." Eden was on her feet and plundering through the large medicine chest Creevy had placed on Theo's desk. She arranged a mortar and pestle and tapped the contents of a small bottle into the mortar. The butler placed a battered metal chalice on the desk and removed the metal lid affixed to the top of it. Eden used a tiny silver spoon to sprinkle a small portion of the mortar contents into the chalice. She gave it a stir and hurried to Theo's bedside.

"My lady, don't go near him," Mrs. Styles snapped. "He's *naked*." The last word came in the housekeeper's version of a whisper. Theo wanted to laugh, but he hurt too much to even try.

Eden sat on the edge of the bed and, with a mere nod, had Creevy lever Theo up whilst he stacked pillows behind his back to support him. "Sir Theo is my husband, Mrs. Styles. There is no scandal in my seeing him naked."

"Married all this time to a strapping man and this be the

first time you've seen him naked. *That's* a scandal," Mrs. Styles muttered, none too softly.

Theo snorted and glanced up at Eden. She rolled her eyes and held the pewter colored cup to his lips.

"Drink."

"What is it?"

"*Tartarised antimony.* A purgative. Drink it." She pinched his nose closed and pushed the rim of the cup between his lips.

He had no choice but to swallow. The concoction tasted of metal, ashes, and sour wine. "That is vile," he gasped, once she removed the cup and used the flannel to wipe his face. "How quickly does it…never mind."

He leaned over and gave way to a series of retches so violent, only Eden's body next to him kept him on the bed. It crossed his mind this was perhaps the most lowering moment in his entire life. His wife stroking his hair whilst he attempted to cast up his accounts was not the way he'd first imagined himself in bed with her. All the while his suspicions about Lowestone and the true purpose of the pasties chilled him to the bone. His stomach granted him a momentary reprieve, and he collapsed back onto the pile of pillows once more.

"Creevy. Who delivered the pasties?"

"Sir?" The butler bent closer to Theo's rusty ghost of a voice.

"How did they arrive?"

"A boy, sir. In a gig from The Grapes."

"Theo, you must rest," Eden commanded.

"Send Jobs to The Grapes. This instant. I want…I want to know…who prepared…"

"Sir, it is three in the morning," Creevy said.

Theo grabbed the butler's arm. "Someone tried to poison your mistress. Send Jobs. Damn—" Still clutching Creevy's sleeve, he bent over the chamber pot. And earned only dry, empty retches for his trouble.

"I'll go, sir." The butler tugged his arm free and quit the room with a few quick footsteps and an uncharacteristic shout to the footman in the entrance hall.

Eden helped Theo back onto the pillows. She glanced at the chamber pot and frowned. "It isn't working. All that noise and nothing."

"Terribly sorry," Theo mumbled. "Hate to disappoint…" His belly continued to roil, but an acute weariness came over him. *Must not sleep.*

"It isn't working, Mrs. Styles. The antimony cup isn't working." Eden leapt to her feet and paced the carpet between Theo's bed and the desk. He fought to keep his eyes open, to watch her float back and forth—a vision in white. Her voice was edged in fear and concern. Concern for him. How long had it been since anyone had worried over him?

Eden stopped at his bedside and touched his forehead. "We must send for the physician."

"You've said yourself, my lady. None will come. The things you had me bring from the still room. Can they not help?"

Theo turned on his side to better to see Eden's face. Through the fog of cramps, nausea, and his throbbing head, he saw how frightened and unsure she was. His heart turned over in his chest. She moved to the desk and picked up several objects one at a time. Her hands shook.

"I can't," she cried softly. "I am no physician." She glanced at Mrs. Styles, who had moved to place an arm around her shoulders.

"Eden." Theo took a deep breath and said it again, louder this time. "Eden."

She walked to his bed as if walking to the gallows.

He took her hand. "I trust you."

She squeezed his hand between hers as if she'd never let it go.

"I trust you." He willed her to meet his gaze, to believe him, to understand. He drew their clasped hands to his lips and kissed her knuckles. "I need no other physician."

Eden drew in a shaky breath. She shook her head. "You are a fool."

"Your fool."

Once she decided to do something, his Lady Grindon did not waste time. Mrs. Styles had put a kettle on his fireside hob when she'd returned to his chamber. Eden mixed water from the kettle into a mug to which she added a few lumps of sugar. She opened a labeled apothecary jar and ladled two heaping spoonsful of its powdered contents into the steeping sugar mixture. She stirred it so long, Theo thought she might put the spoon through the bottom of the earthenware cup.

Finally, she squared her shoulders, turned, and brought the concoction to him. He struggled to sit up and sniffed the contents of the mug.

"What is it?"

"*Carapichea ipecacuanha*, the root at least. We have several of the plants in the conservatory. Drink it before I change my mind." She held the vessel to his lips with trembling hands. He covered those hands with his and tilted the cup to drain its contents.

"That wasn't too bad by half, Lady Grindon. I suspect you — Damnation," he groaned and collapsed over the side of the bed.

Searing pain tore at him, producing retching he felt from the soles of his feet to the top of his head. He was aware of Eden and Mrs. Styles arguing. He'd be damned if he cared to know why. His body had a mind of its own, and he had no choice, save to cede control to whatever foul demon was in charge. No dry retching here. Theo had no idea how long the brutal spasms went on, but he was fairly certain he was casting up food he'd eaten as a child.

"Is it supposed to be this bad, my lady?" Mrs. Styles inquired. "He's been at it rather a long while. I'll have to empty that chamber pot if he goes on much longer."

"Please, Mrs. Styles," Eden pleaded, as she rubbed Theo's lower back in small, light circular motions.

"Not to worry," Theo croaked, waving an absent hand in the ladies' direction. "I'll die soon, and it'll all be over." He was only half in jest. His body went cold. The coals in his belly settled to a low simmer. His throat burned, and he was gasping for breath. Slowly, he lifted his upper body back into the bed.

"How do you feel?" Eden asked, as she worked to settle him back onto the pillows. "You mustn't lie flat. Here, let me. Don't go to sleep. Not yet. Theo? Theo!"

He roused to cold water being dashed in his face. "What the—" Theo flailed his hands and tried to clear his fuzzy vision. He did not need to see in order to smell and feel the comforting presence of his wife, bent close to him, wiping his face and murmuring nonsense.

"You must stay awake a while longer. Just a while longer, then you can sleep. *Shhh.* Lie still. We must rid your body of all the poison."

Theo groaned. "Can't…anything else…I've cast up…my damned toenails…."

"Sir Theo!" Mrs. Styles horror made him want to laugh. He hadn't the breath or the strength. He needed to do something.

Danger. Poison.

Eden laughed softly. The vice gripping his chest eased.

He fought off the need to sleep and tried to sort through the ideas flitting about his brain.

Mrs. Styles's shuffling steps crossed to the chamber door,

where she bellowed Charlie's name. In a trice, the young footman arrived, out of breath and tripping over the threshold.

"Better now, sir?" he asked hopefully, as he reached Theo's bedside. Theo could only offer him a pitiful wave.

"Please take the chamber pot and dispose of the contents as you did the pasties, Charlie. Take a pitcher of water and some vinegar to wash it out over the contents before you bring it back here."

"Burn the-the-"

"Yes, Charlie. As I said." This was the Eden who was mistress of Longbow, the woman who sent Theo notes about tracking dirt into the library. She was still worried and more than a bit afraid, but she did not intend anyone to know.

A blurry figure—Charlie, no doubt—retrieved the chamber pot from the floor and left the room with more care than he had entered.

"Mrs. Styles, bring me that fresh pitcher of water and those extra flannels, then find your bed. I'll see to my husband."

"I'll not leave you alone with a naked Scots botanist, husband or no." The housekeeper plunked onto his bedside table and dropped a few flannels onto his chest.

"Oh, for pity's sake. He hasn't had his way with me in full health and wearing naught but a robe. Naked and weak as a foal, he is far less dangerous."

"That's rather insulting," Theo mumbled as his eyes drifted closed.

"*Hmpf!*" A slide of slippers on carpet and some rather colorful aspersions of Theo's character heralded the housekeeper's departure.

An abrupt quiet settled over his bedchamber. Eden's delicate fingers plucked the flannels from his chest. Less than a minute later, a dampened cloth swept over his chest, up and down each arm, and low over his belly. Then he heard it—the shaky in and out sawing of his wife's breath. He summoned his ebbing strength. At last, his eyelids rose and he forced his eyes to focus on her face. Teardrops clung to her lashes like morning dew on leaves. All color had fled her cheeks. Her chest fluttered against the thin fabric of her night rail partially visible through the gap of her flannel robe. He trapped her flannel wielding hand against his chest.

"Eden."

She tried to continue her ministrations, but he held fast. "That was not amusing," she said, finally looking at him. "Not amusing in the least."

"Casting up one's accounts seldom is, once a man reaches the age of twenty-five or so."

"Of course, it isn't." She swiped at her eyes with her free hand. "That isn't what I— Oh, never mind."

Every word took an effort, but he was determined to allay whatever was causing these cracks in her armor. Not because he minded, but because she did. "What is it then?"

"I should not have given you the *ipecacuanha*. It isn't— I could have killed you." She gave a dry hiccup of a sob and shook her head.

"You didn't."

"I have no business dispensing medicine." She stood and tried to walk away.

Theo tugged her hand and she stumbled back onto the bed, sprawled across his chest. "You have every business. Why do you hold your skills so cheap?"

"Skills? What skills?"

"As a physician, Eden. I know." He drew her braid over her shoulder with his free hand. "I know."

"You're a fool, Theo Grindon. And you mustn't speak of dying. Not even in jest." She snatched her braid away and slapped at his hand. She shoved at his chest for good measure.

"I will not die."

She punched his shoulder. "Why did you say that?" *Punch.* "Why did you eat those pasties?" *Punch* "Why did you fight Lord Lowestone?"

"It wasn't much of a fight."

"It is not amusing, damn you!" She swung at him once more.

He caught her fist with his free hand and brought it to his lips to kiss. "I will not die."

"I had enough trouble finding a man foolish enough to marry me. I'd play the devil finding another."

He pulled her arms around his neck until they were nose to nose. "I *will not die.*"

"What do you know?" she accused in a wobbly voice. "You're a b-botanist." She lay her head on his shoulder and burst into tears.

He settled his palm against the back of her head and drew the counterpane over them both. "I will not die, Eden." Theo held her long after the storm of tears left her body. He held her until the steady cadence of sleep's deep breaths took her. Only then did he whisper, "I promise."

He didn't know what he was promising her. Not truly. Nor did he have the slightest idea what he wanted to promise her or why. This marriage for a greenhouse and a place to sleep grew more complicated and disturbing by the day.

From the time he'd taken his first mistress, he'd placed women in a specific little niche in his life. And they'd fit until they tired of him. Then he'd simply moved on, which made him a bastard of a man, but an honest one. But with Eden… something had changed, and he was having the devil's own time sorting it out. However, for the present, he had a little matter of being poisoned to sort out.

The day's events flowed through his mind as he plucked bits and pieces like flotsam from a river: the physician's journals in two hands, Madame Huang's words, Lowestone's insults, poisoned pasties. Something else pricked at his memory, as his stubborn wife moved closer against him in her sleep. His eyes drifted closed, even as he pondered that missing piece.

THE MUFFLED CLANK AND SCRAPE OF THE FIRE BEING MADE UP awakened Theo from his slumber. His body hurt as if the young maid at the hearth had beaten him with the iron poker. Theo had slept rather soundly despite the night's excitement. Nothing could account for it save—

"Eden." He sat up and searched the disheveled bedclothes for his wife.

Creevy rose elegantly from the chair at Theo's bedside. "It is nearly ten, sir. She awoke at nine and went upstairs to her chambers. She asked me to watch over you until she returns."

Theo slid back against the pillows piled high across the headboard. He drew the counterpane to his waist and smiled at the downstairs maid who, having built up a cherry blaze in the hearth, gathered her tools, curtsied, and left the room with a sideways glance at Longbow's stern, immaculate butler.

He needed a bath, clean clothes, and a cup of tea. Theo doubted his stomach, so empty now it echoed, would accept more than that. He needed to find his wife. But first...

"What did you discover at The Grapes?" Not terribly subtle, but he had no time for subtlety.

Creevy raised an eyebrow but uttered not a word. He retrieved a silver salver from Theo's desk and placed it on the bedside table. It appeared to contain the day's post, but atop it sat a folded piece of parchment. With a glance at the butler, Theo opened the parchment and read the scrawled message. Beneath it lay an innocuous letter sealed with a plain dot of sealing wax and addressed to his wife. Watching Creevy's face the entire time, Theo opened it, read it, and wadded it into a ball.

"Send for Lady Grindon," Theo ordered as he swung his legs over the bed and pushed to his feet.

Creevy coughed and stared at him expectantly.

"Right," Theo agreed, swaying slightly. "Not a good idea. I'd like a bath, then I will seek an audience with my wife."

"Excellent, sir. I will have Charlie and Pip attend you." The butler bowed, retrieved the rest of the post, and walked to the chamber door.

"Creevy, assign one of the other footmen to watch over Lady Grindon."

"Already done, sir."

Theo sat down hard on the bed. He was still weak as water, but he had no time to waste. A sudden movement from the open library door caught his eye. Linnaeus padded into the room and jumped onto the bed where he flopped down and began to clean himself. Theo reached over and scratched the beast behind his ears.

"You are fortunate I would not allow you one of those pasties when you tried to steal it, my friend. You'd be battling with pangolins in the hereafter." He lay across the bed, his arms outstretched. "Which is where I may end up, once I ask my wife why she has been lying to me."

CHAPTER 9

"Thank you, Peggy. I'll soak a bit longer, but then I must dress for the day." Eden closed her eyes and leaned her head against the back of the high copper tub set before the fireplace in her bedchamber. "What there is left of it."

"It is barely half ten, my lady," her young lady's maid chided. "There is still plenty of day to be had, and Mrs. Styles said you had precious little sleep last night." She placed a thick bath sheet, a flannel, and a few face towels on the stool next to the tub and gathered up the nightgown and robe from the hearth rug. "We're proud you saved Sir Theo, my lady. Your father, God rest his soul, would be, too."

Eden refused to open her eyes. She had no desire for her loyal maid to know the turmoil her words stirred in her soul. Those who served at Longbow had done so for years, and some, like Peggy, from childhood. Their adulation of her father was evidenced by the fact no whisper of the true manner of his death had breached the walls of the house.

"Fortunately, Sir Theo has the constitution of an ox," she said after a time.

"Another of my finer qualities?"

Eden sat up and twisted toward the door from whence the question came. She twisted so quickly that she slid under water and came up spluttering. Peggy squeaked and dropped the clothes she'd gathered. She scrambled about and snatched one of the face towels to hand it to Eden. However, the maid appeared so stunned by Sir Theo's arrival in the bedchamber she could only hold the towel out in the general direction of the tub and stare at him.

He strode across the room and took the towel from Peggy's fingers. "Thank you, Peggy. Might I trouble you to beg a few pieces of toast and a pot of tea from Mrs. Deeds? I'll take it in Lady Grindon's sitting room."

"Yes, sir." Peggy bobbed a curtsey, snatched up every article of Eden's clothing—*drat her*—and dropped another curtsey for good measure before hurrying from the room.

Theo came to stand beside the tub but, to his credit, kept his eyes fixed on Eden's face. He handed her the face towel and dragged a tufted leather ottoman over to sit beside her. Eden scrubbed the water from her eyes and resisted the urge to drape the rough fabric over her breasts beneath the water. And he knew it, the scoundrel.

"Good morning," he murmured as she drew her knees up to her chest.

"You should still be abed." Despite her best intentions, she reached out to trace the dark circles beneath his eyes. "You're pale." She placed the back of her hand against his neck. "And your skin is damp and cold."

He pushed a loose strand of her hair behind her ear. "You're beautiful. And I have only just left my own bath."

His hair was damp and draped over the embroidered collar of his banyan. His pallor did not hide the natural golden hue of his skin. Half-dead a mere few hours past, his wide chest and shoulders hummed with vitality. Her fingers trailed down the narrow *V* where the halves of his robe met.

Once she realized his eyes were following her every move, she snatched her hand back and gave herself a good mental shake.

He is not here for this. You did not marry him for this. Whatever this is.

"I am happy you are well enough to climb the stairs and visit me in my chambers," she started.

"No, you're not."

"But I'd like to leave my bath now and—"

"Good." He stood and retrieved the large bath sheet from the stool, opening it wide. "I'll play lady's maid." He shook the sheet in invitation.

"I would prefer you did not." Such a liar. Her body tingled in anticipation of his touch.

"You've seen me naked, Eden. Turnabout is fair play." He grinned at her over the bath sheet.

"You were desperately ill and hardly made a good impression." Eden tried to discern how to use the flannel and the face towel to cover herself.

"I shall endeavor to do better next time. Stop wasting time, Lady Grindon. If you remain in that water much longer you will become pruney. Also not good for making an impression."

"Oh, for heaven's sake." Eden erupted from the water and rushed from the tub, giving her husband her back as he wrapped the bath sheet and his arms around her.

He pressed a kiss to a spot behind her ear that provoked an immediate shiver. "You have the most exquisite *arse* in England, Lady Grindon. *Umpf!*"

He dropped his arms and took a step back, and Eden turned to find him rubbing his side where her elbow had made contact. They both raised their heads at the noisome opening of the door into the sitting room next to Eden's bedchamber.

"Your breakfast has arrived," Eden said, as she walked toward her dressing room., trying not to look back. "Enjoy." Her leave taking would have been far more effective and dignified had she not tripped over the bath sheet and nearly given him another view of her *exquisite arse*.

"I will wait for you to join me."

"I broke my fast earlier."

"And I know who sent you the poisoned pasties." He turned and sauntered into her sitting room, closing the door behind him.

Eden stared at the oak panel between her bedchamber and her sitting room. Her skin still burned where he'd kissed her. She'd awakened this morning in his arms after one of the most deep and untroubled night's sleep she'd ever known. Of course, the press of his hot, sculpted body against hers had sent her from awake to fascinated to enticed in the blink of an eye. Once she'd checked him for fever and felt the steady beat of his pulse, she'd slipped from his bed before the temptation to climb atop and wake him with kisses won out.

She groaned and scrubbed her heated face with her hands —and almost lost her bath sheet covering. It did not matter. She wanted to know what he had discovered about the pasties. With no choice left, she retreated into her dressing room and strapped herself into a set of front-lacing stays, a chemise, sensible wool stockings, and her favorite black and green wool walking dress. Her only concession to being in her own chambers were the black wool slippers she donned and the hasty knot she twisted her hair into before fixing it atop her head with a dozen or so hairpins.

With a roll of her shoulders and a smoothing of her skirts, Eden marched into her sitting room. Only to skid to an abrupt halt inside the door. She took in the chamber in a series of broken glances. The tea table before the hearth bore a tea service, a rack stacked with toast, a small pot of butter, another of jam, and a plate of bacon. Having leapt to his bare feet at her entrance, Sir Theo stood with a cup of tea in one hand and a half-eaten slice of toast in the other. However, it was the contents on the chair and in old boxes on the floor across from him that drew her eye and denied her the ability to look away. She paced to the chair and gathered up the notes she'd locked in her desk.

"You had no right." She stamped her foot and several of the notes fluttered to the floor. She knelt to retrieve them, and in an instant, he was beside her, taking the notes and placing them on the tea tray. Eden tried to snatch them up again.

Sir Theo covered her hand. "I've read them all, Eden. Including the one that arrived in the morning post."

Her heart sank. *Creevy, the traitor.*

"Sit down. Have a cup of tea." He guided her to the chair, scooped up all the notes, and deposited them in a small wooden chest on the side table next to the chair. "Then you can tell me why you have been lying to me all this time." He dropped into his chair and set about preparing her tea, with two sugars and a splash of milk, just as she liked it.

"Perhaps you might tell me why you broke into my desk like a thief and why"—she waved at the larger boxes, each full to the top with her father's journals—"you dragged all these into my sitting room."

He handed her the tea, his long fingers brushing the back of her hand as he did. "I did not break into your desk. I finessed the lock. Completely different. And at least one of these boxes was already in your sitting room. The one containing the latest journals, in point of fact. The one you purloined from *my* library."

She was being managed. Worse, she was being managed by a man against whom her defenses were beginning to slip for the most ridiculous of reasons. And for reasons she had no desire to ponder, she could not allow him to do so. Her pride could not take it. She wanted him to…respect her, to regard her the way he was regarding her now. Competent. Capable. Intelligent. Desirable. *Oh, hell and the devil.*

She took a long draught of tea and placed the cup and saucer atop the box on the side table. "Why are you doing this?"

"This?"

"Reading my post. Studying my father's journals. Attempting to solve a mystery where there isn't one. What business is this of yours?" She stood and turned to walk away.

He grabbed her hand and tumbled her into his lap. "You *are* my business, Lady Grindon. All day, every day. 'Til death us do part."

She snorted and gave a half-hearted shove at his chest. "Nonsense. Managing my personal affairs is not part of our bargain."

"You have personal affairs with the Duke of Arden?" He curled a possessive hand around the curve of her waist.

"Of course not."

"Some other peer of the realm is sending you threatening notes?"

"He isn't…I don't want to talk about this, Sir Theo. I really—"

"Theo."

"What?" She found it impossible to speak when he fixed those green eyes on her face.

"I insist all women who have shared my bed call me Theo."

"I didn't want—"

"And I didn't want to spend my first night naked in bed with my wife retching into a chamber pot like a green boy after his first visit to the local tavern, but we each have our cross to bear. You've chosen to bear your father's, and I want to know why." He gripped her shoulders and guided her around so they were face to face. "Someone tried to kill you, Eden. Someone threatened your father and is now threatening you. I want to know why because that will confirm who."

"To what end?" A vision of her husband drawing Lord Lowestone's cork came to mind. "You have said it yourself. The person who poisoned the pasties is most likely of good Society. You cannot go about accusing a person of rank of trying to kill me. It simply isn't done."

"It simply isn't done." He ran his hands up and down her arms. "Neither is marrying a woman for her conservatory, but that is precisely what I have done. And I do not intend to lose you. I'd play the devil finding another woman with a large enough glass house, a genteel enough reputation, and a lack of standards to marry a scoundrel like me."

Heat radiated where his hands held her, but rather than warming her, his touch sent shivers of anticipation racing through her body. His gaze slowed her blood and pooled its flow in places where she'd not felt it in a very long time. Eden wanted desperately to gather her wits, which flew about her head like feathers in a windstorm. A windstorm made of smooth, marble-hard muscles barely covered by a silk banyan. He was dangerous. A man capable of a singular, rapier purpose always was. She had to steer him away from that purpose or risk losing the one thing she suspected might be more precious than anything else her life had afforded.

"You are not a complete scoundrel," she said, and discovered she meant it. "You do have—"

"A few fine qualities?" He traced one forefinger across the furrows in her brow. "I don't take tobacco. I have the constitution of an ox."

And all the temptation of my every wicked dream.

She gave a tiny gasp as the pad of his finger drew down her nose and came to rest on her bottom lip.

"Not to mention the appetite of a cavalry regiment," her words came out on a thread of breath.

His eyes darkened. "I'm hungry now, Eden."

"You always are." Her body coiled, every sinew drawing tighter and tighter, an overstretched bow string about to snap.

"I shouldn't be. Not like this." He framed her face with his hands. "I will keep you safe. For that, I need to discover the truth. There are only so many obsessions a man can indulge in at once."

"Botany is your obsession. Stick to that and let the others go." Eden lay her hand on the lapel of his banyan and then slid it along the side of his neck.

"That is the trouble with obsessions. All too often a man does not choose his obsessions. His obsessions choose him." He touched his lips—firm, hot, demanding—to hers. He tasted of tooth powder, fresh mint, and raspberry jam. He lifted his head, met her gaze, and waited.

"What obsessions have chosen you...Theo?" She was becoming someone else, a woman she did not recognize. Or perhaps one she did not want to recognize.

"Botany, my whole life." He kissed the line of her jaw. "The truth, since I found the first note threatening your father," he whispered in her ear, then gave her earlobe a sharp nip. "And from the moment you insisted I eat three meals a day, *you*, Eden Turner Grindon. A dozen times a day and all through the night. Against my every preserving instinct. *You.*"

"It *would* have to do with your stomach." She wound her arms around his neck and seared her lips to his. His laughter vibrated against her as he lifted her in his arms and carried her across the sitting room and back into her bedchamber.

"You should put me down. You've been ill." Her protest, a half-hearted one at best, belied the sense of safety mixed with an awakening of every nerve and sinew. An awareness of his strength and what unleashing that strength might be like.

He kicked the door closed between the two rooms. "I am feeling much better now. Must be the toast and jam." He winked.

"Of course." Eden considered the advantages of marriage to a man whose grin should be declared a mortal sin. Unable to resist, she kissed the kicked-up corner of his mouth. A tremor went through him. His eyes darkened further, the color of a fir forest in winter.

"Well," he murmured as he allowed her to slide down his body until her feet rested on the thick Aubusson carpet. He caught her hands in his and the look he gave her had her toes curling in the practical woolen slippers. "I have been ill, and you have made it abundantly clear ours is to be a marriage in name only."

"Do you equate that with illness or being poisoned?" Eden lowered her head, suddenly shy. She locked their fingers together and ran her thumb across his roughened palm.

"Perhaps a little of both. But Eden," he bent to kiss her forehead, her nose, her cheeks, and chin so she had no choice but to fix her gaze on his face once more, "once I climb onto this bed with you, I do not know if I am capable of leaving you untouched without...something breaking in me. I want you more than I have ever wanted a woman in my life, and I am not certain I know why. If you tell me you do not feel the same, I will go back below stairs and drag those journals into my conservatory with me."

"Theo—"

"After I take a swim in the coldest body of water on the estate."

He was giving her the chance to say no, to walk away and keep the plan she'd always had for this marriage, for any marriage, intact.

Without...something breaking in me. How could anything break a man like this? He'd survived war, and loss, and the mercurial whims of women who used him far more than he used them. She knew what it was to be used by someone simply because they could, by virtue of position or fortune. There were so many lies between her and her bartered husband, but in this much, at least, she'd be truthful.

"You do not need to swim in cold water after having been ill. I would not want you to." Though he did not move, she sensed him drawing away. She was bungling this. "Theo, I am not...I haven't remained...untouched." A wave of shame and, yes, sorrow washed over her. She released his hands, but she refused to hang her head.

"Better and better," Theo replied.

He threaded his fingers in her hair, launching hairpins to the floor in a sporadic cascade. His thumbs caressed the edges of her face and came to rest on either side of her jaw, tilting her head up for his kiss. A kiss of such perfect sweetness and strength she wanted to weep. Soft, warm, with a sense of leashed power she longed to draw into herself.

"We came to this marriage with no expectations save those that brought us together. I'll not bring any into it now. In this moment, Eden Turner Grindon, you are every perfect thing I have ever wanted. I only expect you shall let me give myself to you as I am. And that is all I shall expect of you. Agreed?"

Eden cupped his cheek, raised up on her toes, and kissed him. With that, every restraint between them broke. He snatched her into his arms and set his nimble fingers to work on the tapes and buttons at the back of her gown. In her haste, she tightened the knot in the sash of his banyan, then struggled to untie it.

Once she undid the knot, she ran her hands beneath the embroidered silk lapels and pushed the garment off his shoulders. It pooled at his elbows but left the entire front of his body bare.

And what a body he had.

His efforts to undress her faded to a mere awareness as she allowed herself to take in his bare feet, his muscled calves. She shook her hands free of the sleeves somehow gathered at her wrists. Her dress fell to her waist. It was of no matter. She ran her hands up the marble hard tops of his thighs, over his hips and across the ripples of his abdomen. His breath caught and hers caught in answer. He tugged at the laces of her stays. She glided her hands over his chest and shoulders.

A quiet voice inside her uttered a single word. *Mine.*

When she looked up to meet his gaze, a heated flush raced from her toes to her fingertips. Instinct forced her to look down…there. Then she could not breathe at all.

"Oh, my." An idiotic thing to say, save for no other words came to mind. She heard her stays tossed to the floor.

He chuckled darkly. "Is that a good *oh my* or…"

"Good," she said, her voice a husky tone she'd never heard before this man walked into her life. "Quite good."

"Another finer quality?" He lifted her hands from his chest and turned each so he could press a kiss to her palms.

"Fishing for compliments, Sir Theo?" She wore nothing but her chemise and her plain wool stockings, yet she knew neither shame nor fear. The rightness of it all rolled around her like a song.

"Theo." In a motion too quick for her to take in, he whipped her chemise over her head.

"Theo," she whispered.

He slid his hands over her shoulders and down the outside of her arms. The texture of callouses and sinews created sparks of sensation over her skin. His fingers danced along the inside of her arms, tickling the crooks of her elbows. He drew the backs of his hands down her sides, his nails cool and burning all at once. He gripped her waist and rubbed the place where it joined the jut of her hipbones.

Her blood slowed in her veins and grew more heated by the moment.

"You're beautiful, Eden." A dark, erotic thread ran through his words.

"I've been told I have a fine arse."

"I'm not looking at your *arse*."

He wasn't. He was looking into her eyes as if there were some great and wonderful secret there that he wished she might tell him. He lifted his palms to her breasts, brushing over them, back and forth.

She shivered as her nipples puckered in response.

He kissed her left collarbone and kissed his way across her chest to her right. All the while he shaped and cupped her breasts to the point she had to hold onto his shoulders to keep from crumpling to the floor in a liquid pool of pleasure. His lips moved over her body until he reached the place she wanted them.

"Oh," she gasped.

He licked one nipple and then the other. She moved one hand to cup the back of his bent head as he took a taut peak into his mouth and drew on it so hard and long she saw sparks behind her eyelids. He swept one arm behind her knees, still suckling and nipping her breasts back and forth, and pushed aside the bed curtains Peggy had drawn at some point to place her in the middle of the bed. He crawled over her, braced on his hands and knees, until he brushed her damp chest with his and undulated his body so that every part of him touched every part of her.

He touched his lips to hers. A featherlight kiss at first. A nip of the cleft of her top lip next. He drew his tongue across the seam of her mouth. She opened to him, tangling her tongue around his, which elicited a groan from him, deep and shaking with need. He was a man who liked to kiss and whose skill had her writhing beneath him and begging for more, even as she clasped her hands to the back of his head and held him there as if they might draw air from each other and never need to stop.

When he broke off the kiss, he rested his head between her breasts, panting so his breath teased and tormented her aching nipples. As if he sensed her need, he pressed a kiss to each before he continued his kisses down her body, down her belly to the apex of her thighs.

"What are you— Theo, what are you doing?" She pushed up on her elbows as he began to nuzzle the hair covering her sex.

He glanced up and grinned. "Something wicked."

"Oh." Her mind could not grasp the various forms of wicked that came to mind. Then again, she was in bed with her husband in the middle of the day. She was naked save for her stockings, which seemed more decadent than being completely naked. Thank goodness for bed curtains. *To the devil with it!* "Well, so long as it is wicked, carry on."

"As my lady commands."

Eden's mind went blank as he ran his tongue up her cleft. He licked. He nibbled. He found a spot she'd only touched in her most hedonistic moments and he tortured that spot until her body took over and rode up, pushing against his seeking mouth, begging and pleading for him to stop or to never stop. Or to release her into bliss or oblivion, she cared not which. She fisted her hands into the counterpane and rode the waves of sensation up, up, and into an explosion of lights, joy, and freedom so exquisite, she knew no word to name it.

Theo drew his body up hers like an archer drawing a bow, stopping to kiss and nip along the way. He buried his face in her hair and breathed her name. She did not know how, but her arms rose to wrap around him. Never had she been so replete with the sweet weariness that came over her. Her knees rose to cradle his hips. Her feet, of their own volition, planted on the counterpane as her core sought him, rocking against his flat belly. Little shivers danced between her legs to her breasts and down her legs.

"More, my Eden?" he whispered as he adjusted their bodies to meet in that age-old joining.

"Yes, please," she murmured.

"*Hmm.*" He settled himself at her entrance and entered with infinite slowness, his breaths short and heavy against her damp skin.

Eden shifted as her every nerve awoke to his possession. He filled her perfectly, and she reveled in every inch, wanting all of him, and needing him seated inside her. She pushed up with her heels, and he groaned so long and loud she had the urge to laugh at the thought of who might hear them. Their hips met, and he spoke her name. Not a whisper, not a question.

"Eden."

She opened her eyes. He laced his hands with hers. His eyes, green and deep and as enticing as any fairy wood, called to her. She had no power to look away. He began to move inside her. It wasn't enough. She moved against him, awkwardly at first, and then with him as if they were one being. She matched him thrust for thrust, quick and then slow, until they answered each other in a language it seemed only they spoke and had always spoken. Eden tightened her clasp of his hands as the pleasure spiraled in her up and up until she had no idea how it might go higher. Her heart pounded against her ribs. She could not catch her breath, nor did she want to.

Never in her life had she felt so frail yet so strong. He fed her soaring sensations and she fed his. He held her gaze until those sensations overtook him. His eyes closed and his head went back. Faster and faster, his hips met hers until her name issued from his lips with a shout, and heat suffused her, sending her over the waves after him. So powerful was the assault on her senses, for a moment she feared she'd fainted. Until he collapsed on top of her with half groan and half something like a laugh. He kissed her cheek and wrapped her hair around his fingers, still panting to catch his breath.

"If you are laughing at me, sir, I shall make certain this is the last time you bed me or any other woman." She shoved at his shoulder. "Get off me, you great lummox."

He rose up on one elbow and shifted so he was half on top of her. "I was not laughing at you, my Eden. I was thinking."

"Thinking what?"

"Oh my." He grinned.

"Oh my?"

He brushed her hair out of her face and brushed his thumb across her cheekbone. "A good *oh my*. The best *oh my* of my life, in fact."

"Don't be ridiculous." She was weak enough to take great pride in his words, though she did not believe them for a moment. But she wanted to. Desperately. This warmth, this tie to him. She wanted it to last forever.

"What made me think I could marry a woman like you and not make love to her?"

"A woman like me?"

Make love? Oh, she'd not think on that, not now. Not ever.

"Beautiful. Too clever by half. Brilliant. Strong. Sharp-tongued. Sweet."

Eden snorted. "I have already allowed you into my bed. There is no need to turn me up sweet now. I know my charms, meager though they might be where men are concerned. Neither my charms nor my virginity was enough to tempt the second son of an earl, let alone a man of your prowess, in bed. Not after my father was accused of murder."

"Prowess?" Theo made a great show of stretching and flexing his body to its best advantage. "Yet another finer quality?"

Eden punched his chest. "Don't preen. Especially as I realize now how inept... Lord, how inept my previous lover was."

"And who made you aware of his ineptitude?" Theo dropped a kiss to the curve of her breast.

"Fishing for more compliments?" Eden snuggled against his side. He was warm, like a heated brick.

He put his arm around her and drew her closer still. "What is his name?"

"His name?"

"This second son of an earl."

"Why?"

"Curiosity?"

"Theo."

"A man with such poor taste is in need of a good thrashing."

"Absolutely not. I forbid you to thrash another man on my behalf." She poked her finger against his ribs. "Swear it. On your honor."

He sighed. "If you insist. He did do me a favor. Had he married you, I'd be wandering the streets of Edinburgh in search of..." He studied her. She wanted to turn away, but he looked at her as if willing her to see the unspoken words in his gaze.

"In search of?" Why she needed to know, now of all moments, whilst she lay naked in his arms, she refused to contemplate.

"Home."

Home. Oh. She'd done all this to distract him. That was all. Not to...

"You did not swear," she blurted.

"Swear?"

"Swear you will not go about thrashing men who have offended me." *No matter how much my foolish heart desires it.*

"Very well. I swear on my honor I will not thrash men who have offended you."

"There. That didn't hurt too much, did it?" Eden dragged the counterpane over them. She wanted to sleep, and she wanted to sleep in his arms.

"Only my pride." He turned onto his side and tucked her in against him.

"I daresay you will survive it."

"I survived being poisoned. So long as you are near and willing to dose me to within an inch of my life, I will survive anything."

"Don't say that." The warmth and comfort she'd stolen in his arms began to seep away.

"It's true. You are your father's daughter. Both of you have given yourselves over to healing people. I'll not let anyone threaten you for something beyond any person's control. The duke's heir was sick. He died. No one is to blame. And I intend to prove it."

Eden's heart froze. Not only had she endangered her own clarity about her marriage, she'd done nothing to distract Theo. In fact, she'd made him more determined to defend her. Which would be lovely if it weren't so dreadful.

"There is no way to prove it. It doesn't matter, Theo. We are safe here at Longbow. I have no intention of leaving the estate again. I have already warned Creevy and Mrs. Styles to exercise caution when ordering things from Town. We—"

"The truth is important, Eden. Maybe the most important thing there is."

Eden wanted to weep. "How do you plan to find the truth, you stubborn ox of a man?" She laughed feebly.

"After I take a little nap and exercise my *prowess* again, we'll discover the truth together and put the matter to rest," he declared.

He would. She knew he would not give up until he did. One of the many reasons she was coming to…love him.

And she would do all in her power to keep him from discovering who had really killed the duke's son.

CHAPTER 10

His Eden was still keeping secrets.

Theo gazed down at his sleeping wife and resisted the urge to touch the bare shoulder peeking from beneath the counterpane. In the last fortnight, his addiction to the velvet softness of her skin had grown to near obsession. One he suspected would only grow more powerful as the months and years passed. Best to let her sleep. He drew the bedclothes over the delicate porcelain temptation, plucked his robe from the foot of the bed, and belted it as he crossed the bedchamber and went into her sitting room.

His Eden.

When had she become his? The day she'd written the first note, chiding him for not eating the food Mrs. Deeds prepared for him? She'd have him think it was so as not to offend Longbow's despotic cook. God forbid he realize she was managing and caring for him the way she did every single man, woman, child, and living creature under her charge. Was it when she'd wept at the thought of losing her armored pet? She'd gone with Theo to London in spite of her misgivings. Well-founded misgivings, but she'd endured them for St. George.

He could not point to a certain day or time when he'd begun to think of her as his. Nor did he understand the why or how of it. Almost two weeks ago now, he'd nearly died, and she'd saved him. Not many memories of that night had stayed with him. Those that did, he'd never forget. Flashes came to him when he watched her go about her day. She'd lain in his sickbed with him and slept no more than a few minutes at the time. She'd bathed his face and put her palm over his heart to assure herself it still beat. She'd touched her fingers to his lips to feel his breath, and her tears had fallen on his neck and chest.

A more foolish man might believe she'd become his the first time he'd joined his body to hers. He was no fool. At least not where this woman was concerned. They'd made love more than three dozen times in the last fortnight. They'd slept in the same bed, taken their meals together, gone over her father's journals together, and behaved in every way as man and wife. But that was not why he'd come to see her as *his*. It was a puzzlement and one he dared not ponder for long today. Not when she yet kept secrets from him, used her body to distract him, and—

"Oh, sir, you startled me." The upstairs maid, Lettie, stood before the hearth, hands clasped to her bosom and eyes wide. She curtsied. "I'm dreadful sorry, I am."

Theo crossed the carpet and retrieved the maid's pail and tools from where she'd dropped them. He'd been sunk so deeply in thought he'd neither noticed her presence nor heard a sound when she'd dropped her things. So much for his attentive, scientific mind. It had become a confectioner's jelly upon meeting Eden. And turned to mush the night she'd taken him to her bed.

"No need to apologize, Lettie." Theo subsided into the

high-backed chair before the fire and began to sort through the journals and papers on the long, low-set table between his chair and the matching one opposite. "You might, however, make it up to me..." He glanced up at her and saw the conspiratorial smile he'd expected.

"One of Mrs. Deeds' Sir Theo Breakfast trays, sir?" She curtsied again and headed for the door with the pail of tools, coal scuttle, and all. "Right away."

"You're a treasure, Lettie," Theo called after her. Her laughter and the rapid patter of her running feet made him smile.

He reached behind him and withdrew a small leather portfolio he had secreted inside a slit he'd cut into the chair upholstery. The finely cut line in the flowered fabric concealed a hollowed space the size of the worn, folded item in which he kept those notes he was not ready to share with Eden. The notes he surmised she was not yet ready to see. Messages from Madame Huang. The note from the tavern keeper at The Grapes as to the identity of the person who'd ordered the poison pasties. He flipped through the cut pieces of parchment, dated and numbered to match her father's physician's journals. *Her* journals. Now to persuade her to admit the truth.

"Charming the maids again, husband?"

Startled, Theo leapt to his feet, dumping his diminutive portfolio onto the carpet. He scooted it under his chair before he turned to greet his wife. She was pinning up her hair, clothed in his green silk banyan, her gray wool stockings, and her shabby wool slippers. Her eyes, still a bit sleepy, and her skin aglow—she was exquisite. *His Eden.*

"Merely asking that a simple breakfast be sent up, my dear."

"Don't you *my dear* me, Theo Grindon." She evaded his attempt to take her hand and settled into the chair opposite his, tucking her feet beneath her and ignoring the contents of the table. "And your simple breakfast requires two footmen to bear it up the stairs."

He braced his hands on the arms of her chair and bent to deliver her a lingering kiss. She tasted of tooth powder, and her lips clung to his—sweetly, sensuously, and far more enticingly than was good for him this morning.

"Eden," he said, as he forced himself to return to his own chair. "What do you know about an apothecary named Tolliver? His shop is on Bruton Street."

She stared at him, her eyes narrowed, and then she sighed. "You have had another message from Madame Huang."

"Yesterday evening before dinner." He plucked the brief missive from the table and handed it to her.

"You have waited until now to tell me?" She studied the message with care. She licked her lips and swallowed hard. Rather than alluring, Theo found it painful. She'd been forced to keep so many secrets that her secrets had begun to keep her. He wanted to give her joy and passion and…happiness. *Happiness.* As if he could.

"I tried to tell you last night when we took dessert in your library."

"What stopped you?"

"You. When you turned me into dessert." For pity's sake, he sensed the slow creep of a blush along his neck and up to his hairline.

She laughed, a rare yet merry birdsong of a sound. "I must admit, you were a most delectable treat covered in crème."

"I remember the crème being damned cold, and then you took advantage of me. After which I remember nothing at all."

"Liar." She stuck out her tongue.

He strode over the low-slung table in one step and was on

his knees in front of her chair, grabbing at her feet in an instant. "Vixen."

She batted at his hands, laughing this time in a low, sultry voice. A scratch at the sitting room door was the only thing that prevented Theo from dragging her onto the carpet before the hearth.

"Saved by the breakfast tray," he muttered, as he reluctantly returned to his chair.

"God forbid tupping your wife come before the dictates of your stomach," she said with a look of mock innocence.

"Such language, Lady Grindon." Theo gathered up the papers and journals from the table and deposited them on the marquetry table next to him.

Under the high-handed supervision of Lettie, Charlie and Pip set about bedecking the tea table with covered dishes of breakfast foods, the lids lifted to display all of Theo's favorites—a rasher of bacon, eggs, beefsteak, and oatcakes. A rack of perfectly toasted bread accompanied by one pot of fresh butter and another of raspberry jam were set on the marquetry table to one side of Eden's chair. The pot of piping hot tea and its accoutrements finished Mrs. Deeds' offerings.

"Do you require anything else," Lettie asked as Theo began to fill his plate. "Milady? Sir?"

"No, thank you, Lettie. This is certain to keep Sir Theo from starvation for at least an hour or two." Eden buttered her toast and cast a gimlet eye at him.

Charlie and Pip snorted as Lettie shoved them toward the door, trays in hand. The door shut behind them. For a few moments, Theo and Eden turned their attention to making selections from the covered dishes. Eden made herself busy preparing a cup of tea for each of them. All the while, she sneaked glances at the note from Madame Huang, eyeing it as if she expected it to rise up and bite like a rabid hound.

"We have gone through nearly all the journals," Theo started, after he'd quaffed half his cup of tea and held it out for her to refill. "We have gleaned every bit of information they contain about your father's treatment of the duke's heir."

The spout of the teapot clinked noisily against the rim of his teacup. Eden's shoulders rose and fell as she took a deep breath. "Can we not finish our breakfast before you begin the inquisition anew?" She returned to her toast, the slice now slathered with butter and jam, and took a savage bite from it.

"There is no inquisition, Eden. Simply an effort to prove your father's treatment was not responsible for the boy's death."

"You declare his innocence with such certainty." Her bitter tone broke his heart. And told him more and more his latest assumptions were the right ones. Which made her efforts to thwart him frustrating as the devil.

He was weary of this dance. Theo forked a piece of beefsteak and, whilst he chewed it, rose to retrieve the bound periodical he'd tossed onto the settee across the room late yesterday afternoon. He returned to Eden's side and dropped the collection of medical research articles from Edinburgh into her lap.

"Where did you find this?" she demanded. "Who said you might pilfer my private library?" She dropped her toast onto her plate and almost upended her teacup in her haste to stand and shake the offending piece at him. "You had no right, Theo. No right, at all." Still clutching the periodical, she began to pace from the fireside to the settee and back again. Her eyes shone with tears.

Theo went to his chair and retrieved his private portfolio and notes from where he'd kicked them. "I am no physician, Eden, but I can read the latest research of a Scottish physician, especially when it concerns the use of foxglove in the treatment of heart seizures. And from the notes made in that article, so can you."

"I'm not going to listen to this nonsense." She flung the periodical at the settee and turned as if to head out the door.

He clasped her hand before she could leave the room. "You must listen." He handed her his portfolio. "It is all in here. I have taken down every note we've collected. I've added my notes from the Scotsman's research and your comments on that research. I have the contents of every mysterious missive you've received."

Her hands shook as she sat down and began to page through his portfolio. Still, he pressed on. She'd given him no choice.

"Eden, you are determined to find fault with your father's treatment of the boy. There was none."

"You don't know that," she whispered. "You know nothing."

"I know someone in the duke's household shares your need to find your father guilty. Arden's butler was seen ordering pasties at The Grapes. That same man was seen at a number of apothecaries in London in the weeks before Arden's heir died. Tolliver is known to provide his high-born patrons with medicines about which he knows very little. Do you understand what that means?" He clasped her hand. "Look at me, Eden. I am trying to save you."

She snatched her hand away, rose, and dropped his portfolio onto the settee. "You are here to secure my fortune, nothing more. I did not ask you to save me. I did not ask you to prove anything." Her face was white. Her jaw set. "My father's pride and assurance he knew best led him to use a little-known medicine, and a boy paid for it with his life. When faced with what he'd done, the great Dr. Turner took his own life rather than face the consequences of his actions."

"And left you to face those consequences," Theo snapped,

as he rose to face her. "To face someone who is determined to make you pay for what was a horrible tragedy. One in which you are blameless. I won't let that happen, Eden. I cannot." He reached for her once more.

She stepped back and raised her hands to ward him away. "There is plenty of blame to go around, Theo. It is rather like raspberry jam." She drew a handkerchief, his handkerchief, from his silk banyan and wiped a red sticky stain from the lapel of his rope. She wore the banyan far more elegantly than he ever had. "Once it is there, fair or not, it is damned hard to wipe away."

"Only if you choose to deny the truth." He took the handkerchief and tenderly blotted the tears leaking from the corners of her eyes. "My grandmother always said the only thing worse than blaming others unjustly is unjustly blaming yourself."

"I-I'm not blaming myself. Eat your breakfast and return to your plants." She spun on her heel and marched back toward the door into her bedroom, then turned to show him the face of the Miss Eden Turner who'd sent Sir Stirling in search of a convenient husband. The woman accustomed to shouldering the entire burden of Longbow and all its secrets. "We have exhausted the subject of my father's innocence. Nothing we say will change what people think. So long as we stay here and stay vigilant, we shall be safe."

"You truly believe that, my Eden?" He wanted to hold her, to sweep her into his arms and tell her he knew everything. She was not yet ready to hear it, and there were things he was not yet ready to say.

"I am my father's daughter. I have no choice."

He stared at the door long after she'd entered her bedchamber and closed the heavy oak panel behind her.

"I do," he said.

He tugged the bell pull and went to her desk where he

scribbled a hasty note and sealed it with a drop of wax. He dropped into his chair before the fire and continued his breakfast. He was, in the moments his wife did not turn his mind to mush, a logical and scientific man. His study of botany, begun at his grandmother's knee, had made him such. It was time to admit what he'd known for some time now. He'd hoped Eden would trust him with the truth. It meant everything to him, even if he refused to give voice as to why.

"Well, you certainly made a right load of bollocks out of that, Theo," he muttered.

It did not matter. He'd put an end to the threats against Eden with or without her approval. They had the rest of their lives to sort out the rest. If she wanted to. Sometime in the last few weeks he'd discovered, against all odds, he wanted to be her husband in more than name and body.

God help him if she did not want the same.

"I shall crawl across that bridge when I come to it."

A rap at the door reminded him he'd called for a footman. "Come in." He attacked another piece of bacon.

Charlie stuck his head in the door. Theo waved him over and handed him the sealed missive he'd penned. He held up a finger as he chewed and swallowed the bacon. Finally, he was able to speak.

"Please deliver this and wait for a response."

Charlie looked at the direction scrawled across the front of the letter. His eyes widened.

"You do know where—"

"Yes, sir." He bowed. "Of course, sir." Another bow. He turned and hurried toward the door.

"Charlie?"

The footman rounded, eyes wide once more.

"Bring the response directly to me."

The lad nodded and slipped out the door.

It would take a while for Charlie to make the trip to the heart of Mayfair and back. If he did what he wanted, Theo would find his wife to apologize or somehow mollify her. Preferably in bed.

In her current state, however, he might well be in danger of bodily harm. Especially once she learned what he'd set in motion with the errand he'd dispatched her favorite footman. Best to finish his breakfast and retreat to his conservatory. Most men might object to his choice of the word *retreat*. When it came to his wife, Theo suspected he'd be using the word often. Very often.

THEO DREW HIS WATCH FROM HIS WAISTCOAT POCKET AND checked the time. He had lasted nearly the entire day. He'd caught up on his work in the conservatory. He'd spent a great deal of time arguing with Linnaeus over the plump, ornate goldfish in the fountain at the far end of the glass house.

"Lady Grindon will have us both sleeping in the stables if you harm one of her precious fish, you furry menace." As Linnaeus had taken possession of one of the more comfortable chairs in Theo's library as his bed, it was no idle threat. A bribe of cooked trout from Mrs. Deeds' kitchens had settled the argument.

"It is a wise cat who prefers the luxury of cooked trout to the trouble of catching and eating a disagreeable fellow who might fight back," Theo assured his feline friend.

"Pity George has no taste for fish," Pip said as he watched the pangolin digging inside his dirt domain. "Do you think the ants bite him, sir?"

"Wouldn't you if a four-legged suit of armor tried to eat you?"

"I take your point, sir." Pip retrieved the pewter plate

from which Linnaeus had dined and made to leave the conservatory. "Best have this back to Mrs. Deeds. She'll have us both if it goes missing."

"Perish the thought." Theo closed his journal, reseated his quill in the pen rest, and returned his plant samples to their assigned shelves. "Whilst you are there, inquire as to whether Lady Grindon has ordered dinner in the dining room or in her sitting room, will you? I'm famished."

"You, sir? Fancy that," Pip replied with a grin.

"Off with you and your impudence." It struck Theo how differently the servants treated him compared to Longbow's mistress. Yet, it did not trouble him, at all. In fact, he'd begun to think of them and her as family and Longbow as his home. *His* home.

"Oh, you might have to wait a bit for your dinner, sir. That girl, Tilly, took a visitor up to her ladyship's sitting room."

"A visitor?"

"Yes, sir. A real lady. London sort, turned out with a bonnet and a veil and all." Pip gave him a smart salute and scurried off in the direction of the kitchens.

Theo sorted through the detritus on his workbench until he found the response Charlie had fetched from the London address earlier that morning. He read it again, carefully this time. The letter contained no mention of Sir Stirling's wife coming to speak with Eden. He strode through the library and into the entrance hall. His Scots matchmaker might not have mentioned it, but perhaps having another woman speak with her might make Eden more amenable to confronting the Duke of Arden about the actions of his butler and whomever in the duke's household held that worthy's leash.

He took the stairs two at the time and followed the corridor to Eden's bedchamber—his bedchamber of late. If he was to greet Sir Stirling's wife, a duchess no less, he needed to don a morning coat and a neckcloth, at the very least. His hands pressed the door latch, only to find it locked. He tried the other. The same. Why would she lock the doors? He shrugged and continued down the stone floor to her sitting room. This time he pressed both door latches at once, and again, neither gave way.

The hair on the back of his neck began to prickle. In the back of his mind, every bit and bob of information he'd gleaned from the threatening notes—from Madame Huang, from the tavern keeper—began to swirl and jiggle in and out of place.

He pressed his ear to the space where the double doors met. Voices, two different voices. Eden's and someone else's. He knocked on the near door, struggling not to batter it down.

"I am not receiving at the moment," came from behind the door.

"Eden, sweeting, it is me." She'd kill him for addressing her as such if his suspicions were indeed unfounded. But if they were not… "Mrs. Deeds has sent me up to inquire as to your plans for dinner."

"I am still furious with you, you great lummox. Go away. The box of pasties you fetched from The Grapes are here. I shall dine on those should I become hungry."

Damn!

"I thought we might eat those together, my love." He glanced up and down the corridor in search of anything he might use as a weapon.

"You should have eaten them last night. Now go. I refuse to fight with you over pasties through a locked door." The slightest of tremors had crept into her voice.

Hell!

He forced himself to walk back toward the stairs. Creevy

crossed the entrance hall. Theo nearly fell down the stairs in his haste to reach him.

"I need to get into Eden's sitting room. Are the doors the only way in?"

"I beg your pardon, sir?"

He grabbed the startled servant by the shoulders. "The doors are locked. There is someone in there with her. Someone who means her harm." Panic rose in him. He pushed it down and turned to head back up the stairs.

Creevy grabbed his arm and dragged him toward the kitchens. "This way, sir. The servants' stairs. There is a door set into the far wall of the sitting room."

They raced into the kitchens, startling Mrs. Deeds and everyone therein into a hushed silence. The butler went to the area behind the giant hearth and opened a simple wooden door which revealed a narrow, worn staircase. Theo started up the steps, Creevy close behind him.

"Send for Sir Stirling James, Creevy. See to it yourself. Then send for the magistrate."

"The magistrate, sir?"

"Yes," Theo snapped, as he lit a taper from a lamp inside the door. "I'm about to murder someone."

CHAPTER 11

Eden pressed her forehead against the cool, sturdy wood of the door and did her best to choke back the terror threatening to steal her breath. Surely Theo had understood. At this very moment, he had to be formulating some sort of scheme to come to her rescue.

"I was curious as to how you'd survived my little gift, Miss Turner. It might have saved us both a great deal of trouble had you eaten the pasties."

With the meager scraps of calm she yet maintained, Eden turned to face her visitor. Seated as regally as any queen and dressed head to toe in elegant, funereal splendor, the white-faced woman with the pale blue eyes might have been any lady of consequence come to congratulate her on her recent marriage, if not for the Manton pistol clutched in her bejeweled hand.

"I can think of no trouble you and I might have in common, Your Grace." Eden flattened her hands against her kerseymere gown but refused to clench the soft fabric, no matter how badly she wished to do so.

"On the contrary." The duchess lifted the portfolio Theo had left on the settee earlier. "According to this, you and I have a great deal in common." Her eyes took on an odd, flat affect. Her lips thinned into an almost feral smile. "I thought to make you pay for what your father did to my son. If what is written here is true"—she flung the portfolio, scattering its pages across the thick carpets like leaves from a late autumn tree—"you—"

"I am the one who suggested my father dose your son with foxglove." Eden marveled at the steadiness of her voice even as she slid one foot back beneath her skirts.

She stood little chance of running for her bedchamber door before the pistol cut her down. She'd be damned if she'd go down without a fight. She'd live with the guilt of what she'd done, but over the last several weeks, she'd discovered a good reason not to die over it. A reason she hoped might come crashing through her sitting room doors at any moment. She slid the other foot back. Somewhere behind her the fire poker stood in its stand, if only she might reach it.

Had she known the Duchess of Arden had been allowed to cool her heels in the sitting room long enough to discover Theo's suppositions, Eden would have fled the house and taken every breathing creature in it with her. Her fury at Theo discovering her secrets and saying nothing counted as naught against the murderous intentions of a duchess driven mad with grief. She'd deal with her husband's perfidy later. The quandary of the moment lay in thwarting a madwoman's quest to make someone, anyone, pay for the loss of her son. With her eyes fixed on the duchess's face, Eden wiggled another inch closer to the hearth.

"I can scarcely credit it, Miss Turner," the duchess said, as she rose gracefully from the settee. "Sitting here waiting for you to attend me, had I not read it myself, I never would have dreamed your father was so foolish as to allow a mere girl to make decisions about my son's care."

"Truly, Your Grace?"

The voice steadied her heartbeat and warmed her to her toes, despite the icy sweat rolling down her back.

The duchess turned and leveled her pistol at Theo, who had suddenly appeared across the room behind her. Eden stumbled back. Her entire attention had been so trained on the lady with the gun she'd not realized he had entered the room until he spoke. Fortunately, neither had the Duchess of Arden.

Theo, hands clasped behind his back, executed an abbreviated bow. "Why would you take issue with Lady Grindon prescribing your son's medicine when you yourself sent your man to fetch more of that selfsame medicine without Dr. Turner's knowledge?"

"How dare you? Do you know who I am?" Her Grace's hand began to shake the tiniest bit.

"You are the woman who has been trying to kill my wife for something for which she bears no blame." He stepped toward her as if they were in a Mayfair ballroom discussing the weather.

With the duchess's attention riveted on Theo, Eden backed between the tea table and chair and reached behind her until her fingers touched the cool metal of the fireplace poker.

"Dr. Turner put my son in danger the moment he listened to the ignorant discourse of his empty-headed daughter. They murdered my son with their duplicitous quackery," she shrieked, as she turned and aimed the Manton at Eden.

"Quackery, Your Grace? Is that why you chose to ignore Dr. Turner's instructions, find your own supply of foxglove, and dose your son beyond his physician's instructions?"

"He wasn't getting better." She turned to look at Theo then back at Eden once more. "A duke's heir must be strong and vigorous." The veil she'd pushed back over her bonnet threatened to fall into her face. She swiped at it with her free hand, which caused the pistol to dip. "Your father swore he would make him well and he murdered him. *You* murdered him!"

Behind the duchess, Theo's eyes widened. He stepped to the back of the settee. His glance fell to Eden's right side, where she grasped the poker behind her skirts.

"Down," Theo mouthed, as he gripped the back of the settee with both hands.

Like a single drop of rain suspended from a tree branch, the moment hung motionless. The fire crackled and spit. The Duchess of Arden's breath rasped in and out of her twisted mouth. Eden's heart thundered in her chest. Her blood whooshed in her ears.

"No, Your Grace," Theo said. "You were desperate to please your husband. You bought the medicine. You dosed your son, and it killed him."

Eden dropped to the floor, flinging the poker across the room to catch the duchess across the knees.

"Liar!" Simultaneously, the duchess half-turned toward Theo and fired the Manton.

Theo leapt across the settee and carried the duchess to the floor with him. The scent of smoke and gunpowder permeated the room. Eden crawled across the floor and retrieved the poker to bring it down across the duchess's free hand as she wrestled with Theo for control of the pistol. The duchess snatched her arm back in pain and elbowed Theo in the nose. Theo roared and flattened himself atop the duchess, spreading her hands wide beneath his. Voices from the corridor and pounding on the sitting room doors began to rise.

A wailing scream from the Duchess of Arden, like an animal cry, chilled Eden to her bones. The Manton fired again, then skittered into the wall as if it had a will of its own.

"Fetch the gun, Eden," Theo gasped. "The gun."

Eden rose to her feet to do so as the doors burst open. Creevy, Mrs. Styles, Pip, Charlie, Mr. Jobs, and Sir Stirling James spilled into the room.

"I see Grindon has it all in hand." Sir Stirling crossed the room and pried the pistol from Eden's locked fingers.

Charlie and Pip clapped their hands over their ears to block the duchess's screams. Eden wanted to laugh until Theo lifted his head to look at her.

"You're bleeding." She snatched the cloth tucked into Mrs. Styles's pinafore and tried to kneel next to her husband and the still struggling duchess.

"Get back," Theo ordered. "She bites. And she broke my nose."

"I'll take her,"said a quiet, cultured voice near the sitting room doors.

As one, the occupants of the room—save for the sobbing duchess—turned toward the voice. Lord Lowestone acknowledged Sir Stirling with a nod and strode toward Theo, who got to his feet, drew the duchess up from the floor, and settled her onto the settee. Her bonnet dangled down her back. She wrapped her arms around herself and set to rocking back and forth with wide, deadening eyes.

Theo stepped between Eden and Lord Lowestone and curled one arm back as if to cage her there. "The duke's butler swears you had nothing to do with this," Theo said. "I will have your word on it."

Eden took one step to the side, still behind Theo's arm, but she needed to see Lord Lowestone's face. To watch events she'd never have imagined in her wildest imaginings unfold. The young lord turned to her, his face ravaged and his shoulders tensed as if beneath a great weight.

"My word of honor, Grindon. I had no idea…" He drew in a shuddering breath. "I did not know her grief had taken her so far. You have my word, she will not trouble you again. I will see to it myself."

"Because the duke cannot be bothered," Eden said.

Lord Lowestone's head snapped back. He opened his mouth to speak, glanced at Theo, whose body fairly shook with rage. "Because it is my duty. I owe you an apology, Lady Grindon. I do beg your pardon. For my behavior. For… everything." He offered her a decorous bow.

"Are you satisfied, my lady?"

Eden had never heard Theo's voice so cold, so officious. He did not look at her, only continued to stare at Lord Lowestone. A room full of people and not a soul moved—not counting the weeping, rocking duchess.

"Of course. Did you come in a carriage, my lord?" Eden marveled at her genteel solicitude. Inside, she screamed. At her husband for not telling her he'd discovered all her secrets. At the duchess for her foolish, deadly efforts to please a man who would never be pleased—a man who was happier with a dead son than with a weak but alive one. At her father who had bragged to the duchess about the use of a new medicine, giving the duchess the instrument of her own destruction, and ultimately the instrument of his.

Eden maintained her ladylike tone and posture, with no idea as to what gave her the strength to do so. Or perhaps she did and refused to credit it…or him.

"Perhaps Mrs. Styles might help Lord Lowestone to conduct Her Grace to the carriage?" Sir Stirling suggested in the quiet, steady tone Eden had come to know as his managing voice.

Longbow's housekeeper looked to Theo and then to

Eden. She nodded, and Mrs. Styles and Lord Lowestone helped the duchess to her feet and led her to the corridor. The other servants stepped back with alacrity, giving the trio a wide berth. Eden fought not to smile.

"Lowestone," Theo commanded.

The duke's heir turned at the doors.

"If she comes near my wife again, I will take out advertisements in every newssheet in London and whisper in the ear of every inveterate gossip in Mayfair," Theo declared. "The entire world will know the Duke of Arden's son died due to the misuse of medicine by Her Grace. Do we have an understanding, Lord Lowestone?"

"We do." Lord Lowestone inclined his head and quit the room.

Eden caught Creevy's attention and indicated the other servants. With one word and a look, he ushered Charlie, Pip, and Mr. Jobs out, after they'd offered Eden, Theo, and Sir Stirling each a bow.

"I will speak to the duke." Sir Stirling took Eden's arm and seated her on the settee, taking a seat beside her. "After I questioned the butler, Lowestone pensioned him off with instructions never to contact the duchess again. She will be exiled to one of Arden's northern estates. Lowestone is a good man, Grindon. He will see it done in spite of the duke's protests. Are you well, my dear?" He patted Eden's hand.

She stood abruptly and took Theo by the elbow. She shoved him onto the settee, retrieved the cloth she'd taken from Mrs. Styles, and wetted it from a pitcher on the sideboard beneath one of the windows.

"I thought it was your duchess," Eden said matter-of-factly, as she tilted Theo's face up to wash away the blood. "When Tilly came into my bedchamber and said I had a visitor, I thought my husband had begged her to come and placate me."

"Ah! It would have been a wise choice," Sir Stirling replied.

"Wish I'd thought of it," Theo muttered.

"Are you often in need of placating where Sir Theo is concerned?"

"Daily," Theo said, before Eden could answer. He hissed in pain as she pressed the damp cloth to his hand where the duchess had bitten him.

"Be that as it may," Sir Stirling said with a grin, "I am pleased you puzzled it out, Grindon. Were you not here, it might have ended differently. I am off to placate the magistrate Creevy so efficiently fetched. Then I am for Arden's. His Grace is the one who made your cousin think he had a right to your inheritance…Lady Grindon." He stood, took Eden's free hand, and bowed over it with his customary flair. "Your father loved you. He had his flaws. We all do. He…left you in a moment of weakness. No one is to blame. Sometimes, our lives are woven out long before we are born. If we're lucky, we find a way to overcome it." He glanced at Theo. "Or a person to help us do so." He released her hand and brushed a bit of lint from his sleeve. "I would tell you to look after each other, but I suspect there is no need."

Even after the door closed behind Sir Stirling, Eden continued to clean Theo's face and wounded hand. She poured water from the pitcher into the basin and rinsed out the cloth. She returned to the settee and sat next to Theo, pushing his sleeve back to better attend the angry bite wound.

"Your cousin?" Theo asked.

"Rupert Throckmorton. My father's sister's son. Dreadful skinny pig of a man. Tried to have himself declared my father's heir even after you and I married."

"Yet another man I must promise not to pummel?" Theo

tried to grin, then grimaced as Eden touched his injured nose.

"No need. Creevy invited Rupert to spy on you whilst you were working in the conservatory the day after we married. Said once Rupert saw the size of you, he decided not to pursue the matter further." She ran her hand up his sleeve to find a scorched hole burnt into the fine linen. "You've been shot!" Eden rose only to have Theo pull her back onto the settee.

"My shirt was shot. She missed me." He pointed over his shoulder. "Hope you have more of this wallpaper hidden away somewhere. Those two holes will have to be covered or Mrs. Styles will have my—"

Eden punched his chest. Repeatedly.

"Wait! What the devil?"

"You could have died, you great lummox."

"Not a chance." He took her in his arms and kissed her hair. "You threw off her aim when you tossed the poker at her. Besides, being a great lummox has its advantages. It serves to take down mad duchesses and to instill fear into skinny, porcine male relations."

Eden flattened her palm against his heart. It beat steady and firm against her hand. She loved him. She'd given him her heart against every instinct she'd honed to a fine point over the years. Even as she admitted it, doubts and fears flickered at the edges of her mind, tiny flames that warned and threatened to engulf her chance at happiness. She'd married him for money and property. She'd endangered his life. She'd kept the duchess's threats to herself because she believed she knew best. As she believed she knew best when she'd advised her father to try foxglove to heal the Duke of Arden's son. And Theo had known. Like her father, he'd known and kept it from her.

"My father told the duchess about the foxglove. He knew

she killed her son." Eden stood and went to the window overlooking the extensive back gardens beyond the conservatory. She needed to see Longbow to see what her marriage, what her father's medical work, had bought. "Didn't he?"

"Yes."

"How long have you known?" She pressed her hand to a windowpane. The coolness soothed her. A bit.

"Since I started reading your father's journals. The ones he wrote, not the ones—"

"I wrote. But you've read those, too."

"You know I have. For the last ten years, every new treatment, every new insight, has been yours. I've seen your medical library, Eden. And I have read your notes on his cases. You are a skilled physician, my love. The career he made for himself in the great homes in London was due to you. Your work. Your—"

"My arrogance. My pride. My foolish belief Papa would not carry his boasting too far." She turned to find him standing behind her. "He carried everything too far."

"Yes, he did, but that is not your fault. None of this is." He ran his hand down her arm. "I should have told you what I knew."

"Why didn't you?"

He shook his head. "It doesn't matter. I know about arrogance, Eden. And pride. And the cost of denying one's passion for the sake of a parent. I paid a terrible price for mine. I lost everything and it *was* my fault."

"I don't understand. Theo, I—" She gave an involuntary gasp as he swept her into his arms and strode to the chair before the fire, sitting with her in his lap.

"All I ever wanted to do was study botany. The only happy moments of my childhood were spent in my grandmother's conservatory. My father found it intolerable. He berated and insulted me and encouraged my brother to do the same, until my pride decided to show them how wrong they were about me."

"You joined the cavalry." Eden tried to imagine an earnest young Theo, shamed into doing something he never wanted. The pain nearly took her breath away. She traced a small pattern at the vee where his shirt opened.

"Bought my colors myself. My grandmother begged me not to go. Said she'd speak to my father, which only pricked my pride all the more. She said she needed me, but it didn't matter. I was determined to go."

"You were young," Eden insisted.

"As were you when you decided to study medicine and aid your father whilst keeping your abilities secret. He depended on you far more than he should have and allowed you to shoulder all the guilt and blame."

"It isn't your fault your family died, Theo."

"I never blamed myself for my parents' deaths. Nor my brother's. But my grandmother…"

"You said she died of typhus."

"She did, but after my parents tore down the dower house and the conservatory and forced her to move into a cottage in the village. She managed to save most of her plants for me. Many of the ones I brought here were hers. She had to leave her roses, and I know it broke her heart. She lived for me, Eden, and for her plants and gardens. I left her alone. They left her to die alone, save for a young housemaid and foot-man. My brother was in London. My parents were warned to leave. They refused. Had I been there, I could have taken my grandmother away. I could have—"

"You could have died of typhus with her."

He smiled against her hair and drew her closer. "And you could have eaten those pasties. You could have lost your home when your father died, but you did whatever you had to do to keep it and to take care of everyone who depends on

Longbow. You helped your father with his medical practice. He is the one that made the decision that led to a boy's death. And his own."

"He left me. He encouraged me to study medicine, and when it went all wrong, he left me." She wanted him to understand. Her reasons for keeping secrets. Her reasons for not trusting him. Her reasons for not daring to believe what she'd reveled in the last few weeks could possibly last.

"But I won't, Eden." He leaned back and turned her to face him. "I will never leave you. I will never be anything but proud of your passion for medicine. I will never ask you to hide who you are from the world. I cannot promise you a life free from troubles or sorrows. I can only promise to stand by you through it all so long as there is breath in my body. I didn't tell you I knew your secrets because I wanted you to trust me enough to tell me yourself. Can you do that, my Eden? Can you trust me enough to live life at my side no matter what happens?" He gazed at her, and for the first time since she'd known him, he looked uncertain and perhaps a bit afraid.

"I do not want to go to London," she said, her mind and heart racing.

"Done. We'll have George's dinner delivered."

"I do not know if I wish to study medicine."

"Agreed."

"But I might."

"Very well."

"I cannot promise to be an obedient or soft-spoken wife."

Theo snorted.

"You will still have to remove your boots before you come into the house from the conservatory. And you—"

He kissed her, long and hard. When she tried to open her mouth to speak, he kissed her again until she thought her lungs might explode. She braced her hands on his chest and pushed. Theo blinked at her, his face serious and somehow dearer than she'd ever believed it might be.

"I love you, my Eden."

"You what?" She lost her balance and nearly fell off his lap. He wrapped his arms around her and squeezed. Not that it mattered. She'd ceased to breathe.

"I love you. You don't have to—"

She pressed her fingers to his lips. "Stop talking."

"Yes, my lady," came his meek reply.

She cupped his face in her hands. He closed his eyes and released the tiniest of sighs. She touched her lips to his brow, his eyes, the sharp blades of his cheekbones. She kissed the corners of his mouth, his chin, his nose.

"You came through the hidden door to the kitchens, didn't you?" Eden whispered against his lips with a wicked smile.

His eyes flew open. "What?"

"Now that you know how to reach the kitchens without being seen, I will never be able to tempt you, will I?"

"Well, I do have a passion for food," he murmured.

"As my larder well knows."

"And for botany." He kissed her once more. "But you will always be able to tempt me with my favorite passion, my Eden."

"What is that, my love?"

"*My love?*" Theo grinned, but his rough tone said so much more.

"I've loved you from the moment you dragged me into the carriage to go in search of George's food."

"Who knew wood ants were the way to a lady's heart?"

"You did, Theophrastus Grindon. Now, what precisely is your favorite passion?"

"If I tell you, will you promise to indulge me in said passion?"

"Perhaps." She ran her hand up his buckskin clad thigh.

He covered her hand and nudged her chin to bring her eyes up to lock with his. "You, my Eden. Until the day I die, my greatest passion will only, forever, always be you."

"That is the way to a lady's heart." She kissed him soundly. "Now, indulge me in my favorite passion and take me to bed."

CHAPTER 12

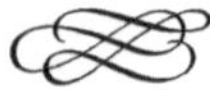

December 1817
Hampstead

A LIGHT TAP ON THE DOOR TO HER NEWLY APPOINTED SITTING room drew Eden's attention from the latest medical journal out of Edinburgh. It had arrived yesterday, as had several others, thanks to her husband's connections.

"Yes?" she answered.

Charlie stuck his head in the door from the entrance hall. "They're here, my lady. Sir Theo is in a right lather about it, too."

"Is he now?" She gave the footman a wink and tossed the periodical onto her reading table. "Run along and tell him I am coming."

With a jaunty salute, the young footman crossed the room and went through the library toward the conservatory. Eden shook out her skirts and slid her feet into her woolen slippers. They had converted the former downstairs bedchamber into a cozy sitting room with all new furnishings—carpets, and wall coverings in buttery yellows and light shades of green—and moved the various pieces left over from her father's medical practice into the upstairs sitting room she now shared with her husband. They often spent their evenings writing up their research there before retiring to the bedchamber for research of a different nature.

She fetched her blue paisley shawl from the back of a chair and swirled it around her shoulders as she went through the library into the conservatory. A familiar scene greeted her. A group of men from the stables and the home farm milled about inside the outside conservatory doors. Mr. Jobs shouted instructions. To make matters worse, Linnaeus had cornered Pip, who was doing his best to climb a trellis replete with bougainvillea. Fortunately, George was happily digging in his box of dirt, oblivious to the impending mayhem.

Head and shoulders above them all, hands on hips, Theo spotted Eden and strode toward her. He bussed her cheek and drew her shawl more tightly around her.

"Please tell me we are not expecting the delivery of more furniture for the sitting room," he pleaded. "I am not certain Charlie, Pip, and I are up to another day rearranging every single item in that room another sixteen times."

She rolled her eyes. "It was no more than half a dozen times, and Charlie and Pip did most of the furniture shifting. This delivery is not for the sitting room."

"Where is it to go?" Theo offered his arm and escorted her to where the men were unloading the contents of a canvas covered wagon. Mr. Jobs directed the men to bring in a series of burlap covered bags and line them up across the wall of the conservatory.

"They'll need to stay in the glass house until spring, my

lady. The cold will be too much of a shock for them, to my way of thinking," Mr. Jobs said, cap in hand.

"I am certain you are correct," Eden replied. "But perhaps we should ask Sir Theo. He is, after all, our botanist."

"Scots botanist," Theo corrected with a grin. "Well, let's see what we…" his voice trailed off as he went down the line removing burlap coverings to reveal thorned bush after thorned bush, their roots incased in a burlap covered ball of earth.

"These are roses," he said softly.

"Nothing gets past himself, does it, my lady?" Mr. Jobs teased.

"He is a clever one, our Scots botanist," she agreed.

"Where did you…" Theo bent to read a handwritten tag preserved between two pieces of glass and attached to a thick branch of the rose bush with a little chain. Eden saw the moment he recognized the handwriting and his expression had her heart turning over in her chest.

"They came from Suffolk. I thought we might plant a rose garden in the spring."

Theo stared at her in stunned amazement. "How did you do this?"

"I can be very persuasive," Eden said with a saucy smile as she turned and walked back toward the library. "I wrote that I wanted your grandmother's roses to bloom here at Longbow this summer to celebrate the birth of her first great grandchild."

"What? Wait! Eden!"

Eden winced as the cacophony of pots crashing, a cat yowling, and a footman sliding down a trellis followed her sprinting husband. He caught her before the French windows into the library. He was laughing and shouting all at once as he picked her up and whirled her to the sound of the servants' shouts and whistles.

"Are you certain?" he demanded, his expression serious and his eyes wide with hope.

"Oh yes, my love," she replied. "You have indulged your favorite passion exceedingly well. Exceedingly well, indeed."

Sneak peek at the next Marriage Maker romance **Reckless Desire** by Tarah Scott

Kenna Ramsay, a peasant girl born out of wedlock, is content to live a simple life with her aunt and cousin on Skye. When a nobleman sweeps into town with news that she is a long forgotten descendant of Robert the Bruce, Kenna can hardly believe it. Until she learns her connection is one out of wedlock. Some things don't change.

Bryson Maxwell, future 4th Earl of Newhall, descends from a line of men known for falling in love at first sight. Bryson respects his lineage, but he has no intention of following in his male ancestor's illustrious footsteps. After all, why should a man love just one woman when there were so many to love over the course of a lifetime?

CHAPTER 1

Bryson Maxwell, the future 4ᵗʰ Earl of Newhall, had grown up being told that he would one day fall madly in love. Falling in love—or more accurately, falling in love at first sight—was a requirement of Newhall men. Bryson slowed on one of Inverness's lovelier park's graveled paths. Affection rippled through him with the memory of sitting on his grandfather's knee while his grandfather described the instant *his* father laid eyes upon Bryson's great grandmother and knew that she would be his bride.

The old man sighed. "It was the same with my own Sophia. She had eyes as green as emeralds. How they flashed when she was angry." His expression clouded, and Bryson just knew that his grandfather had returned to a time before Bryson was born, when the woman he loved still lived.

Bryson hadn't known either woman, but he imagined they indulged their husbands' tales with the same patience Bryson's mother did his father when he recounted how he had seen her across a crowded ballroom one fateful night thirty-two years ago and had begged for her hand in marriage two days later.

The story was enough to induce a man to avoid ballrooms.

Almost.

Ballrooms weren't his problem today.

Bryson fixed his gaze on the woman strolling beside Lady Chastity, twenty feet ahead. From his vantage, he only glimpsed her profile, and the red hair peeking out from beneath her bonnet. That he'd fallen in love with her without fully seeing her face stung his pride. What sort of man decided to marry a woman whose face he had never seen? A fool, that's what sort of man.

He didn't usually stroll in the park. On beautiful early summer days like today, he preferred to ride about his father's estate, where his horse could trot for an hour before reaching their farthest field. Two days ago, however, Sir Stirling James requested that Bryson join him in town to discuss business. A note sent to Bryson's townhouse this morning invited Bryson to meet Stirling in the park. Apparently, Sir Stirling favored morning walks, and a man didn't turn down an invitation from the future Duke of Roxburgh.

The women halted, and the red-headed angel bent to sniff a rose on a bush that crowded the path. Bryson stopped. His heart pounded, whether in dread or euphoria, he wasn't certain. His only chance at escape was to…well, escape. Forget business. Forget Sir Stirling. Board the first ship to France— Nae. America. He would need the two-month voyage to forget the desire that tightened his bollocks to near discomfort. Bryson spun, took one step, then stopped short. Sir Stirling, fifteen feet away, rapidly approached.

"Forgive me, Stirling," Bryson said. "I cannot stay."

Stirling stopped in front of him and frowned. "What is amiss?"

For the first time in his life, Bryson's stockpile of harmless fabrications fled his mind. One learned to bend the truth

—or, at least, avoid it—when ladies were in the vicinity. Now, however, all he could focus on was Stirling's eyes, which shifted past him to… God help him, Stirling had to be looking at Lady Chastity and *the woman*. Stirling's face lit up. Of course. Everyone knew the man was besotted with his wife.

In the next instant, Lady Chastity stepped up beside Bryson with the red-haired lass at her side. Lass, nae. Nymph. He got a good look at that damned hair, and desire caused his cock to twitch. He'd never seen hair dance as if alive with fairies. She was tall for a woman. The top of her head reached the bridge of his nose. Her bloody pelisse dipped low enough to offer a teasing view of creamy flesh. Too easily, he envisioned the lithe legs hidden by her pale gold dress.

"Stirling." Lady Chastity smiled at her husband, then turned to Bryson. "Lord Newhall, how nice to see you."

"My lady." Bryson bowed, forcing his eyes to remain on her.

"May I introduce Miss Ramsay. Kenna, this is Viscount Newhall."

Miss Ramsay extended a gloved hand. "Sir," she said in a low, throaty voice that sent his heart galloping.

Bryson grasped her gloved fingers. His chest tightened when he noted the slight tremble in her hand. Was she as affected by him as he was by her? He bowed and brushed his mouth against her fingers. How he wished she didn't wear those blasted gloves. He caught a hint of lilac and his cock twitched again. God help him. He was about to embarrass himself as he hadn't done since the age of seventeen. He straightened and released her. Now to make his getaway.

"I understand congratulations are in order," Lady Chastity said.

Bryson frowned. "I beg your pardon?"

She smiled. "Your brother is to be married."

"Ah, yes. Thank you." He sounded like an idiot. He was an idiot.

Last week, when his younger brother announced his engagement to Lydia Crawford, the sister of his childhood friend—and the lass Matt had sworn to marry when he was ten—Bryson had concluded that chances favored his avoidance of whatever curse afflicted Newhall men that caused them to fall in love with such abandon. He was the fifth Newhall man and one out of five was decent odds. It seems he'd been wrong.

Lady Chastity turned toward Sir Stirling. "Shall we walk, or do you gentlemen have business to discuss?"

Stirling's eyes softened. "I believe we can spare a few minutes for you ladies."

Lady Chastity shook her head and looked at Miss Ramsay. "Isn't that just like a man? They believe they do us a favor by allowing us to bask in their company for a few stolen moments."

Sir Stirling grasped her hand and brought it to his lips. His eyes locked with hers. "We are the fortunate ones."

Lady Chastity's cheeks pinked, and Bryson thought of his father who, after more than thirty years of marriage, still had the ability to make his wife blush. Might Bryson be able to make Miss Ramsay blush thirty years from now?

His thoughts froze. God help him, it was too late. No power in heaven or hell could get him to board that ship to America. He was going to marry Miss Kenna Ramsay.

KENNA WISHED MIGHTILY THAT SHE HADN'T ALLOWED LADY Chastity to talk her into a walk in Summit Gardens. But the allure of sun and trees had been more than she could resist.

Inverness's park couldn't replace the woods of Skye, but it was still beautiful—despite the grand people who intruded—like the three women who approached.

Sir Stirling and Lady Chastity started away and Lord Newhall winged an arm toward her. Kenna slipped her hand into the crook of his arm before realizing what she'd done. The muscle beneath her fingers tightened as they started forward. She'd glimpsed the tiny smile on Lady Chastity's lips before she and Sir Stirling started walking. Of course, she was pleased the gentleman was being gallant. She was so kind—too kind. That kindness is what had gotten Kenna into this predicament.

They neared the ladies. Kenna groaned.

Lord Newhall looked down at her. "Are you in pain, Miss Ramsay?"

Kenna snapped her head up and met his gaze. He stared down at her, brow furrowed in concern. Had she groaned out loud? Aye, she had. Just one more indication that she didn't belong here. She had to write another letter to her aunt, begging her to allow her to return home. Agreeing to leave Skye had been a mistake. What did it matter that she was one of many descendants of Robert the Bruce? Society couldn't possibly care that she was a Flower of Scotland.

"Miss Ramsay?" Lord Newhall said.

From the corner of her eye, she saw the women stop on the path in front of Sir Stirling and Lady Chastity.

"I am fine," Kenna whispered.

"Lady Chastity, how nice to see you," the short, fair-haired girl said. "Sir Stirling." She curtsied, and the others followed suit.

"Ladies." Sir Stirling, ever the gentleman, bowed.

As one, they rose, and shifted toward Lord Newhall. For him, they dipped so low, their cleavage—one ample, two so modest they could scarcely count as cleavage—were in plain view. The fair-haired woman looked up at him through her lashes. Women vying for a man's attention, Kenna understood quite well. Even in the hills of Skye, women competed for the attention of the most desirable bachelors. Of course, a handsome man like Lord Newhall, whose attire, manners and deportment proclaimed him wealthy, received extra attention.

He angled his head in acknowledgement and, to Kenna's surprise, not only didn't free himself of her hand, but covered her hand with his free one and squeezed. All three pairs of female eyes locked onto the action—and narrowed.

Thank you very much, you lout, Kenna mentally seethed. *Now—*

The girls rose, and Sir Stirling said, "Do you ladies know our guest, Miss Ramsay?"

"We have heard of her, but have not had the pleasure of an introduction," the blonde said.

"Permit me to make introductions," Sir Stirling said.

Kenna murmured greetings, unable to curtsy to the noblewomen, as Lord Newhall kept a tight hold on her hand.

"That is a lovely gown, Miss Ramsay," Lady Fiona, the taller brunette, said. "You are brave to wear such a low bodice."

Kenna blinked. Had the woman just insulted her?

"Do you really think the bodice is too low?" Lady Chastity's brow furrowed. "Oh dear, perhaps I miscalculated when I purchased the dress for you, Kenna."

Lady Fiona's eyes widened. "Not at all," she hurriedly denied. "It is especially lovely on her. The color is very flattering."

"What a relief." Lady Chastity smiled at Kenna. "I want Miss Ramsay to be seen in the best light."

"You always keep a finger on the pulse of current fashion,"

the girl said. "I fear I am woefully behind the times with this conservative dress."

Kenna worked to keep her fury in check. "Lady Chastity's choices are always perfect."

The group turned deadly silent. Kenna's heart raced. She'd done it again. It wasn't her words, but her tone. Gentle Society didn't show anger.

"We all agree that Lady Chastity's choice is perfect."

Kenna started at Lord Newhall's statement.

He smiled down at her. "I think the dress is exquisite."

The stares of the three women burned into her skull.

"You are correct, of course, my lord," Lady Fiona said in a too-sweet voice. "Well, if you will excuse us, tasks await us."

Sir Stirling bowed, but Lord Newhall only watched until the women brushed past them. Lady Chastity and Sir Stirling began walking, and Kenna fell into step when Lord Newhall started forward.

They took half a dozen steps before the silence closed in around her. "Forgive me, Lady Chastity, I was rude."

"Were you rude, my dear?" she asked.

"I was, as you know—but you are too kind to point out my flaws. Which is exactly why I should return home."

"Return home?" Lord Newhall cut in.

Kenna looked up at him. The furrow in his brow had returned and deepened.

"Where is home?" he asked.

"Skye," she replied. "I am only here for a visit."

"When will you return?"

"Tomorrow, if I can."

"Tomorrow?" He halted.

Kenna and Lady Chastity stopped and looked at him in surprise. Sir Stirling, however, clearly struggled to control a smile. What had gotten into the man?

"Perhaps that can be arranged," he said.

Kenna's heart surged with hope.

"Stirling," Lady Chastity admonished.

He blinked at her. "What is amiss, my dear?"

"You know full well—" She broke off and glanced their way.

Lord Newhall's muscle tensed beneath Kenna's fingers. She shifted her gaze to his face, but he stared at Sir Stirling. A group of people came around the path's bend ahead of them—Mrs. Stone and Miss Stone, accompanied by Mister Stone. Kenna had met the down-to-earth family three days past and liked them. Probably because they weren't nobility, she thought with a mental snort.

The family reached them and stopped.

"How lovely to see you, Lady Chastity," Missus Stone said. "Sir Stirling." She and her daughter curtsied.

"We will have none of that." Sir Stirling smiled. "We are all friends here. You know Lord Newhall?"

"We haven't had the pleasure," Mister Stone said.

Stirling made the introductions. Of course, Miss Stone blushed when the viscount bowed over her hand. Something he hadn't done with the previous ladies, Kenna noted.

"I know you remember Miss Ramsay," Stirling said.

Mister Stone bowed. "Miss Ramsay."

"It is wonderful to see you again," Mrs. Stone said. "We are so looking forward to seeing you—and Lady Chastity and Sir Stirling, of course—at our luncheon tomorrow."

Kenna smiled. "Lady Chastity says we will be there."

The two women smiled.

Mrs. Stone's eyes shifted to Lord Newhall. "We would be pleased to have you, as well, my lord."

To Kenna's surprise, he said, "I would be pleased to attend. Perhaps Lady Chastity can provide me with your address?" He turned his smile upon her.

"Stirling has the address," she replied.

Despite his charming smile, Kenna still sensed tension in Lord Newhall's posture. She didn't have to guess at the cause. Embarrassment and regret warmed her cheeks. In less than fifteen minutes, she had revealed her lack of gentle breeding. Like the gentleman he was, he hadn't pulled away from her, but he must surely want to rid himself of her company as soon as propriety allowed. They weren't far from Lady Chastity's parked carriage. She could withdraw her hand from his arm on the pretense that she and Lady Chastity were to return to the carriage. With a deep breath, Kenna pulled her hand free. His head snapped in her direction. His frown deepened.

"Have a pleasant walk," Mrs. Stone was saying.

"We will see you tomorrow, Miss Ramsay," Miss Stone said.

Kenna nodded. "Until then."

The young woman smiled, and the family moved past. Kenna started forward, her gaze straight ahead. Lord Newhall walked alongside her with Lady Chastity and Stirling to her right.

"Stirling, I imagine you and Lord Newhall should get back to your business," Lady Chastity said, and Kenna released a silent breath of relief.

"We have all day for business," he replied." How often do we have the opportunity to enjoy the park together?"

"Quite often, actually," Lady Chastity remarked. "I believe Kenna and I will visit the rose garden." She linked her arm with Kenna's. "Good day, gentlemen."

Kenna glimpsed Lord Newhall's stiff bow in the instant before Lady Chastity turned her toward the rose garden. Kenna had the odd feeling that Lord Newhall stared at her. She kept her gaze forward and concentrated on her steps. She would die of embarrassment if she tripped over her skirt in public, as she had when they'd left the house that morning.

CHAPTER 2

Bryson tried not to stare at Miss Ramsay, but he couldn't tear his gaze away. The sway of her hips wasn't what transfixed him—though his cock pulsed at the hint of round buttocks beneath her dress. Nae, it was simply that she walked away. What if he didn't see her again? What if she left town? He groaned inwardly. He was acting like a fool.

What did it matter if she left town? He could follow her anywhere.

Stirling clapped him on the back. "Shall we go?"

Bryson broke from the spell. "Of course."

Stirling turned. Bryson force himself to follow.

"I hope to finish our business today," Stirling said. "Chastity plans for us to leave Inverness later tomorrow after Mrs. Stone's luncheon. I have many preparations today in order to be able to leave on time."

"Leave?" Bryson looked at him in surprise. "Where are you going?" The words left his mouth before he realized how presumptuous the question sounded.

Stirling flashed white teeth. "Chastity wishes to visit our estate near Lossiemouth."

Bryson's heart stuttered. "Will Miss Ramsay accompany you?"

They broke from the trees and Bryson's horse came into view, one among several clustered about the tying posts.

"Perhaps," Stirling replied. "She received an invitation to the Colonies, where she has family."

"The Colonies?" Bryson blurted. "She said she came from Skye."

"Aye, but she wishes to visit the Colonies."

"That is a long way for a young woman to travel alone."

"I doubt she will be alone." Stirling leaned closer and said in confidential tones, "I doubt she will go at all."

Relief flooded Bryson.

"Several young bucks are pursuing her. I suspect one of them will capture her heart."

Bryson halted. "The devil, you say? Surely, she's not considering their suits?"

"Why ever not?" Stirling asked. "They are respectable young men. Well, one is a tad bit older, but he is a viscount, so that is a strong incentive. Her family would be delighted to have her become a viscountess."

Bryson's heart raced. Which viscount sought a wife? Horror struck. "Viscount Hensley?" He narrowed his eyes on Stirling. "You cannot possibly be considering his suit."

Stirling laughed. "It is not up to me, lad. She and her aunt will make the decision."

"I am no fool, Stirling. Your word carries weight. They will, no doubt, heed any advice you offer."

"Who am I to interfere in her affairs?"

"You are Sir Stirling James, Marquess of Roxburgh, future Duke of Roxburgh."

Sterling scowled. "Christ, man, you make me sound like the Messiah."

"In this case, you are. You have it within your power to save her from a life of drudgery as Hensley's wife."

"I wouldn't call it a life of drudgery," Stirling mused. "Her circumstances would be much improved."

A horrifying thought struck. "By God, you facilitated the match."

Stirling shook his head. "As I said, I hold no sway in the matter."

Bryson worked his hands into fists at his sides. "Encouraged then. I have heard—bloody hell, all of Inverness has heard, and probably half of Scotland, too—how the Marriage Maker makes matches."

Starling laughed again. "You credit me with far too much influence. I have, on occasion, made introductions. That is all."

Memory flashed of a wedding several months ago. He stared in horror. "You had a hand in Lady Buchman's marriage." He had wondered why the marchioness married so suddenly. Bryson's gut twisted. He hadn't given much credence to the rumors that no one in the Marriage Maker's sights could escape. If the rumors were true, that meant the match between Miss Ramsay and the viscount—

Stirling's low chuckle yanked Bryson from his thoughts. "I never took you for a man who listens to idle gossip."

He didn't. Only, what he'd heard about The Marriage Maker wasn't idle gossip.

LATER THAT EVENING, BRYSON ACCEPTED THE FULL BRANDY glass Sir Stirling offered him. "Third time's a charm," he murmured, and took a healthy drink.

"I beg your pardon?" Stirling sat in the chair to his left.

Bryson released a breath and kept his gaze on the fire

burning in the hearth. "I was just thinking that perhaps this glass of brandy might take my mind off things."

"Things?" Stirling sipped his brandy. "We had a successful day. Your father will be pleased."

Bryson nodded. "He is as giddy as a schoolgirl at the prospect of the partnership. He considers shipping one small step away from privateering—which, as we all know, is simply government sanctioned pirating—and he finds privateering a romantic notion."

Stirling laughed. "He isn't completely wrong. Given Napoleon's war, any ship on the open sea risks an encounter with pirates."

"Which is why my mother will not allow him on that ship."

Stirling lifted his glass in salute. "To Lady Newhall. Clearly a woman of sense and intelligence."

Bryson always thought he favored his mother in that regard. Now… He finished the brandy.

"Another?" Stirling asked.

Bryson considered, then nodded. Stirling refilled his glass, again, and again…

At last, the clock struck ten, and Bryson stood. The room swayed slightly. "I believe it is time I take my leave."

"So soon?" Stirling asked.

"My mother taught me never to overstay my welcome."

Stirling's eyes twinkled. "One must always listen to his mama." He stood, and they started toward the door. "Will we see you at Lady Lexington's party tonight?"

Bryson caught himself before he blurted the word 'we,' and said in a casual tone, "'We'?"

"Chastity, Miss Ramsay and myself."

No doubt, Miss Ramsay would wear a silk ball gown—turquoise with a low bodice, like the dress she'd worn that morning. They would dance. He would entice her to walk in the garden, pull her close and taste those full lips—and the sweet rosy peaks of her breasts. His cock began to harden.

"Will you be there?" Stirling asked.

"I hadn't planned on attending."

They reached the open door.

Bryson gave a slight bow. "Thank you for the brandy." He spun and strode into the hallway.

Twenty minutes later, Bryson entered the darkened foyer of his townhouse, stripped off his great coat and hung it on the coat rack to the left of the door. He strode across the foyer to the staircase directly ahead and began to climb the stairs, mind fixed on the full decanter of whisky waiting on the table in his room.

By the time he reached his chambers, he'd half decided to wake his valet and have a hot bath drawn. That and the whisky were sure to put him to sleep. He slowed two steps into the room, his gaze on the hearth's low fire. For an instant, he envisioned Miss Ramsay on the carpet in front of the hearth, red hair glistening in the firelight, arms wrapped tightly around him as he thrust inside her.

"There you are, darling," purred a sultry female voice.

His senses swam. Could it be? But the answer came almost before he truly comprehended the question. Bryson spun to face the naked woman in his bed.

"How did you get in here, Kathryn?"

She stretched like a cat. "I have my ways. Now, come here. I haven't seen you in two days. I have missed you terribly."

Even without the benefit of liquor, he recognized the lie. Mrs. Kathryn Sands wasn't capable of tender feelings, which was the very reason he'd taken her as his mistress—that, and her dedication to pleasing him. He made it a point of honor to return the devotion, along with a generous monthly allowance. There wasn't the slightest danger she would fall in love with him, nor he with her. For her to be here, in his home, without invitation, was a breach of their understanding. She was up to something.

He scanned the room and caught sight of her clothes folded neatly on the chair near the window. Bryson crossed to the clothes, snatched them up, and threw them on the bed.

"Get dressed."

"Darling—"

"Now," he snapped.

Her eyes widened. "Bryce, what is amiss?"

"Pray, do not embarrass yourself further. Innocence does not become you."

She sat upright. "Surely, you are not angry because I am here?"

"Either dress yourself, or I will wrap you in that sheet and put you in a cab."

"You wouldn't dare."

He stared.

Her mouth thinned. She scooted off the bed and, for the first time in their relationship, she didn't tease him when she dressed.

www.scarsdalepublishing.com

Reckless Desire

A Rose in Disguise

The Marriage Maker and the Widows

Rake Ruiner

Marrying the Belle of Edinburgh

Widow's Treasure

Seduction of a Widow

The Beasts of Blackstone Abbey collection

A Heart Worth Loving

A Scoundrel's Promise

A Match Made in the Highlands

Sweet Hellion

Forbidden Love

My Lady My Siren

His Temptress His Torment

Her Unrepentant Rogue

Not Another Knob

The Marriage Maker and the Widowers

The Runaway Baroness

His Imaginary Courtship

Music on the Waters

London Lonely Hearts Club

Beautiful Beast

www.scarsdalepublishing.com